B?

W9-BDH-946

CAPRICE

Lacey Dancer

ZEBRA BOOKS
KENSINGTON PUBLISHING CORP.

ZEBRA BOOKS are published by

Kensington Publishing Corp.
850 Third Avenue
New York, NY 10022

Copyright © 1996 by Lacey Dancer

All rights reserved. No part of this book may be reproduced
in any form or by any means without the prior written consent
of the Publisher, excepting brief quotes used in reviews.

If you purchased this book without a cover, you should be
aware that this book is stolen property. It was reported as "un-
sold and destroyed" to the Publisher and neither the Author
nor the Publisher has received any payment for this "stripped
book."

Zebra and the Z logo Reg. U.S. Pat. & TM Off.

First Zebra Printing: June, 1996
10 9 8 7 6 5 4 3 2 1

Printed in the United States of America

One

"I can hardly believe it, my dear," Lorraine Dayton-St. James said with satisfaction. Her eyes sparkled with delight as she looked to the head of the table where the second of her four adopted daughters sat beside her new husband. She turned to the right, touching the hand of Caprice, her first chosen child, with a smile. "I was so afraid my little plan wouldn't bear fruit. But it did."

Too aware of the stare of the man sitting so silently across from her, Caprice shifted uneasily, trying to mask the movement with a look of interest. He was watching her, had been watching her all afternoon, through the wedding ceremony and the picture taking that had followed. And now here, at the restaurant, he had yet to take his eyes from her face. He might be an associate of Killian's and someone her new brother-in-law clearly respected, but the man unnerved her.

"Caprice, you're not listening," Lorraine murmured, some of her pleasure dying as she studied Caprice's tense face. "Are you all right?"

Pulling herself together, mentally damning the man who was coming between her and her family, Caprice forced his image and impact out of her thoughts. This was her sister Silke's day and she would enjoy it. She focused on her mother's face, trying to make her smile as natural as possible. The searching look she got in return warned her better than any words could have done. She sighed deeply but discreetly. She didn't begrudge her mother her joy, but she also wasn't ready to face any gentle hints in her own direction. Her life wasn't going well at all and she had no intention of telling Lorraine.

"Please, don't count on the rest of us marching down the aisle. Silke has always been one of a kind," she murmured gently.

Lorraine patted her hand, relieved at the response. For a moment, Caprice had looked almost hunted, and that had never been Lorraine's intention. "I'm not counting on anything. But I am hoping. I know you weren't very happy with me when you left Philadelphia. You, more than the rest, were giving up a lot."

Caprice heard the plea in her mother's voice. Lorraine so seldom asked for anything, in spite of all she had given to her and to her adopted sisters, that Caprice couldn't resist offering the reassurance she didn't really feel. "I did give up a few things," she admitted honestly. "But maybe I am a little set in my ways. You think so. Silke thinks so. A year of trying to make it in a totally different environment without the St. James's name and influence as backing should fix that." She leaned sideways to kiss her mother's cheek. "Just don't expect me to come up with a husband like Silke. I don't work that fast. I'm the slow, steady one, remember."

Lorraine searched her eldest daughter's eyes. Of the four, Caprice had been the most angry at her interference. "You've forgiven me?"

Caprice found a smile more easily than she would have thought. "Yes. I was only in a rage for a day or two. But I'm not the raging rebel that you took in any more. I've learned to control my temper. I'll make my year." Being careful not to glance in that man's direction, she looked briefly at her younger sisters, Leora and Noelle, as they chatted quietly two places away. "We all will. You've done a good job even if we still have a way to go."

Lorraine's smile broke. "I'm glad, my dear. I've been very worried. I didn't want to hurt any of you, but I just didn't know what else to do to get you to reassess your lives."

"Asking us to make a complete break for twelve whole months as a birthday present for your seventieth was definitely a novel way to wake us up," she agreed dryly.

Lorraine laughed softly, for the first time believing that her most success-oriented child might be softening just a little from the tough little survivor she had to be to rise above her unstable past, with its endless road of broken promises, midnight escapes, and uncertain futures. "I do my poor best."

Caprice chuckled quietly, unable to resist her mother's humor.

As she tilted her head, her gaze caught his. Her laughter remained, but the real amusement driving it altered.

Randall Quinlan, "Quin," held her eyes, seeing the subtle change in her. Caprice was very good, he decided, watching her carry her part of the conversation even as she reacted to him. She was more than he expected from what little he had heard from Silke, more even than the one picture he had of her. He raised his glass to his lips as she turned away. Wariness. He liked that. He didn't want to think that she would come to him easily. She would not be the woman he had waited for all these years if she did. Although his expression didn't show it, he was amused at the way fate had arranged his destiny.

Repaying the debt he had owed Killian had brought him to Atlanta. Danger had waited in many guises, for Silke, for Killian, and for himself. But they had won. Killian, with Silke wrapped securely in his arms, had stood in a garage with police milling around while he had leaned down to pick up Silke's handbag and its spilled contents. Caprice's face had looked up at him from a snapshot lying in a dark puddle of dried oil. He had stood, staring at it for a moment, unable, at first, to believe it had finally happened. Silke had given him the first clue when she had told him that she had an adopted sister. The next confirmation had been the clench of desire in a body he controlled too well not to know a very strong need had breached his normal barriers. Silke had gotten her handbag back, but he had kept Caprice's picture.

After that, the wedding made it easy to meet her. The picture hadn't lied, but the reality was far better. Caprice was tall, in her heels almost six feet. She wore her height like a queen, her head up, those smoky green eyes direct. But her voice was not regal at all, although she tried to make it so. She tended to break the ends off her words in a vain attempt to disguise the natural depth and easy flow of her speech. There was a whisper quality to her words, the kind of vocal seduction that invited the listener closer. She didn't like the sound as far as he could tell. There was always a faint flicker of a frown whenever it peeked through and she would hurriedly correct it. Contradiction. The lady was definitely that, he decided as he continued to watch her. Suddenly, she turned her head, her eyes narrowing. He waited, feeling the surprisingly strong sexual pull that came with the action. He knew his patience to be limitless when he wanted something. But this woman, the one he wanted more than he had ever wanted anything, was trying that patience with sidelong looks that challenged despite her very clear need to do exactly the opposite.

Caprice held his eyes, determined this time he would be the one to look away. She swirled her wine in the glass she held as she saw his eyes change. The silver gaze was no longer simply intense. A new emotion entered the light depths. Her restless movements stilled, her body froze, held by that look that said "I have you now." No one had ever touched her in the way this man seemed to do with just a glance. He had too much of an effect on her, and she didn't like it. She knew his name. Randall Quinlan. Even that was too much. Just as he was too much. Too tall, at least six feet six inches. Too quiet. Rarely speaking but always watching. Too alert. Each sound and change in his environment was cataloged with those light eyes. Too controlled. No motion was wasted when he moved, no expression expended uselessly, no smile granted just for the sake of convention.

She swallowed carefully. Caught by her own determination not to show weakness, she couldn't look away. The sounds of the party faded. Her world, framed in seconds, was measured in each breath he drew, each shiver of response that slowly, as drops of rain anoint a parched earth, filled her senses. His scent lingered in her mind, spicy, exotic, expensive. His warmth, that one time he had touched her, was an imprint on her skin, lasting too long, an invisible brand to remind her that he had met her flesh to flesh. Primitive. That was the word. Primitive. The reactions. The needs. The man. Herself.

Her eyes widened with the knowledge. She was not a woman for emotional displays, primitive or otherwise. The past had taught her to civilize her reactions, her needs, her behaviors. She was what she had made of herself, successful, socially correct at all times, and in command of her own destiny. No feeling, no matter how unexpected, would make any difference in the end. Her eyes glittering with determination and challenge, Caprice tilted her chin, giving him back his look. The technique never failed.

Until today. Admiration flickered briefly, stunning her. Most men, all men in fact, who incurred her displeasure were quelled when she faced them. Suddenly, the walls she had built over the years seemed more paper than brick. Fear brushed delicately against the thin surface, butterfly wings of long-denied weakness that had the power of a cannon to destroy. Her skin paled in the soft light of the restaurant. Sounds of laughter and voices scratched the silence like claws unsheathed. Her head lifted another fraction, her chin tilting with defiance that didn't erase the fear but somehow made it less damning. His brows rose, a flicker of expression to emphasize those pewter eyes. Acceptance. He raised his glass slightly, toasting her and her challenge.

Caprice followed the movement, shocked at how easily she understood him without a word passing between them. The fear grew, sown by this man whom Killian, her new brother-in-law, called friend, whom Silke made smile when no one else seemed to have the knack. She watched his lips caress the crystal, his eyes holding hers over the rim. The pale liquid imprisoned in the flute slid slowly into his mouth, was held in the warm darkness, savored with the finesse and care of a lover, then consumed ever so delicately. Erotic. Her fingers clenched around her own glass, her lips dry, aching. When he stood, drink in hand, she drew back, certain he understood her need when she didn't understand it herself, certain he was coming to her. Tense, confused, angry, she waited, ready to fight him. For one second he made no move only his gaze monitored her reaction. Then he turned from her and looked to the head of the table.

"A toast," he announced softly in a lightly accented voice that carried gently over the noise and merriment to draw everyone's eye. "To Killian and Silke, who were fortunate enough to find completion in this world of broken dreams and promises. And courageous enough to hold onto their treasure, protecting it with the best of themselves. May your days always be filled with the joy and hope of this moment." He raised his glass.

Caprice came to her feet with the rest of her family, her eyes on Silke and Killian but her mind locked on Quin's words. Poetry and cynicism. A strange combination, like the man. She lifted her flute, watching Silke, her hand in Killian's, get to her feet, the love in her eyes clear for the world to see. Silke had filled the empty places in her life, as always the first of the four sisters to race out to meet life. Even as Caprice felt the first dry touch of rare champagne slide down her throat, she acknowledged that, for her, there would be no such courage, no jump from the world she had always known into the unknown. She took no chances, had no taste for risk or those who leapt blindly into tomorrow. She had to know. She had to believe. She had to have something to hang on to. Emotion wasn't enough. She had learned too well the folly of trusting intangibles. As she sat down again, she consciously didn't look Quin's way again. Whatever the man was to Silke and Killian, she would allow him to be nothing to her.

Quin stood at the back of the group saying goodbye to Killian and Silke, watching each member of Silke's family. Families meant nothing to him, but human behavior did. Emotion had always intrigued him. Logic was truth by perception, predictable, usable. Understand the way a man or woman thought and one had the key to his or her choices. But emotion was the ultimate challenge, the wild card in the dynamics of human decisions. Emotion could give superhuman strength or weaken Hercules. In the seven before him, he saw a little of each. Killian and Silke were made greater by the emotion called love they bore for each other. As were Lorraine and Geoffrey. But Noelle and Leora, the younger St. James sisters, did not seem to have that secret yet.

Lastly, his gaze fastened on Caprice. Nor did Caprice. Caprice with the whimsical name and the no-nonsense look. Caprice with the cool green eyes that analyzed everything and everyone with the precision of a brilliant mind. No emotion lay in that clear gaze, no clouds of doubt, no joy of life such as could be found in Silke's wicked look. But there was no fearful shrinking either, as found in Leora and Noelle. Only logic lived in this beautiful woman with the silver-white hair and curves to bring a saint to his knees in homage. The hair was bound up, imprisoned by a hand that demanded obedience. The clothes concealed, shrouding the body in cloth and secrets. Camouflage. His lips twitched in silent amusement. It didn't matter. He had chosen. He traced the line of her rigid spine, knowing she felt him watching her. She would fight. He understood that. She would use whatever weapons she could lay her hands to. He accepted that as well. She would deny him. Hell, she already had. It wouldn't matter. He looked down at his own hands and the scars they bore. He understood fighting better than she. Understood losing and winning as well. And defenses built with bare hands, agile minds, ingenuity, and desperation.

He looked up and past Caprice for just a moment to see the last hugs and smiles for Silke and Killian just before they stepped into the limousine. Soon they would be at the airport, where his personal plane would take them to their honeymoon on his island. Over the next month he would have no home. Not that it mattered. He had other plans, plans that didn't include returning to his retreat. He glanced back to Caprice as she stepped away from the crowd of relatives and closer to him, once again oddly alone in a family with whom it was clear she shared love. A strange reaction, another facet he intended to explore.

Caprice turned, finding him watching her. Suddenly, the day, the needs that seeing Silke's happiness had generated in her, and his intense scrutiny combined to create a volatile mix. Her temper slipped its bonds. Her eyes glittered with anger, with emotion too long kept under wraps. Her hands clenched as she fought and won against the need to strike out.

"Stop it," Caprice hissed. She could feel his heat surrounding her. She tipped back her head, glaring at him as she had wanted to do since the first time he had looked her over.

Quin gazed down at her, waiting. "Stop what?" he asked quietly.

Caprice felt his smooth velvet voice like a soothing touch down her back. She fought the feeling and the man who conjured it out of nowhere. "You stare at me as if you own me."

"You read people very well."

Not expecting his answer, she inhaled sharply, her eyes widening with shock. "You admit it?" Fear returned, wisps of fright to urge caution, flight. One she could accept. The other she could not.

He saw the fear, surprised by it. For one moment, he doubted. Before he could change his mind, the fear dissolved into anger. "I don't lie." He shook his head, faintly annoyed at himself. "At least I won't ever lie to you."

"You won't get the chance," Caprice snapped back, startled enough to forget to guard her words. She regretted the reply the moment it left her lips, not because of his reaction but because of her own. She hated being out of control. She knew the cost of that kind of reaction, had paid it in the past and vowed never to pay it again.

Quin reached out, his hand encircling her wrist, tracing the pulse that raced beneath the golden skin. "Don't," he commanded. He shook her hand lightly, demanding her attention.

Caprice blinked, focusing on his face, hardly noticing his touch. "Don't what?" she whispered. How could she feel like this? Why now? There was nothing in her life to hold on to, nothing to stave off the uncertainty of her future.

"Don't remember that kind of hurting. It does no good. It only steals light from this moment."

Caprice drew back mentally, and tried to physically. "Let go," she breathed, suddenly realizing he was holding her.

He looked down, opening his fingers one by one, letting her hand slide from his.

Caprice jammed it in the pocket of her skirt, ignoring the warmth that left with his touch. But she couldn't ignore his words. "You don't know what you're talking about."

Her fear was alive and eating at her. His expression gentled. Even when he didn't know the source, he understood the fear as he understood the courage. "I do. One day I will even tell you how I know. But not now. You don't believe me. Or yourself for that matter."

Caprice shook her head, putting a step, then two, between them. "Go away."

"There is a lot I would give you if you asked. But that I cannot do."

"Won't."

He searched her face, seeing the confusion clouding the fear. Before there had been no emotion. Now there was almost too much. So much she didn't understand, didn't know how to control, and yet it was clear she desperately wanted to control, probably had to to survive. A hard lesson. Taught by whose hand? That, too, he would know in the end.

"No, I won't," he agreed. He glanced past her to see the relatives starting to turn, to include Caprice in their conversation. He stepped out of the magic circle even as he looked back at her. "I hurt you somehow. Shall I leave for now?"

"I don't know what you mean. I don't care whether you stay or go." Two lies spoken without thought.

He smiled then. "Courage and defiance. Irresistible."

For one second, Caprice felt that smile as a priceless gift, then her family closed around her. And Quin stayed, talking with her father, charming her mother, and somehow managing to ease Leora out of her shyness. For Noelle, he displayed a gentleness that seemed so natural Caprice found her eyes drawn again and again to his face, looking for something to hang on to, to mark as fact in the paradox she sensed but couldn't touch. She found nothing solid, only more intangibles. Curiosity was a seed. Proximity was the first bud of growth. Then time. Then nearness. So many questions to be asked. But she never did. Her courage, that word he cursed her with, was a bud that never bloomed. Her mind hovered over the flower, tasting its color, its texture, but leaving it on the vine. Tomorrow the sun would come. The bloom would wither with the passage of time and die. As it should. Quin was risk. She understood that if nothing else on this strange day.

Two

"You're avoiding me."

Caprice turned around with a jerk, staring up at Quin's impassive face. She had been so certain she had escaped him. "No, I'm not," she replied swiftly.

He shook his head, cataloging every change of her expression. If she would not let him know her with words, he would make do with what he could discover on his own, at least for now. "I didn't think you were afraid of me."

She drew herself rigidly erect, the gesture bringing her to six feet with the benefit of the low heels she had worn. Not that it mattered. Quin still made her feel small, feminine, and, oddly, on the defensive. All three reactions were impossible to handle. "I'm not," she denied firmly.

His brows drew together faintly as he studied her. If he hadn't been watching every move she had made as the party had broken up, he would have missed her dodge into the ladies' room as everyone else had gotten into the limos to take them back to their hotel. He had intended riding with them. As Killian's best man, it was his job to see that all went smoothly before, during, and after the ceremony.

"Then why did you try to give me the slip?" he asked.

Caprice eyed him, seeing nothing in his stance to belie the impression that he was prepared to wait indefinitely until she came up with a plausible reason. "I simply needed to use the facilities."

"I could point out that that rarely takes forty-five minutes."

Caprice grimaced. "You would have to be the kind to keep track." She sighed deeply, with emphasis. She had hoped to avoid this confrontation with her ploy. All she had succeeded in doing was making herself appear foolish. "All right. You force me to be rude. I didn't want to run into you, and with my family accepting you so readily, that was a lost hope."

He nodded, undisturbed by her admission. It was no less than he had thought. He lifted his hand, encircling her wrist, marking her pulse and the sudden change in rhythm with his touch. The fear was back in her eyes, stronger now, more demanding of his consideration. The reaction hurt, more perhaps than it should. He accepted that, too, as the next step in what lay before him.

"I had promised myself and you honesty. But that upset you, didn't it?" He watched her eyes, finding more truth in them than in her words. Anger diluted the fear. He waited, alert and prepared to adjust himself and his actions to her needs. His reactions were remnants of a long-dead training, so ingrained now that they were as much a part of him as his muscles and bones.

"You think I should be flattered that you all but told me that you own me? What century did you come from?" she retaliated. With the strongest will in the world, she couldn't completely wash the fear he generated in her from her voice. That he admired her looks she didn't doubt. That he watched her with a perception that was as unnerving as it was intent only added to her caution. Yet, despite all she could see, there was too much she couldn't. Hidden depths. Risks.

"I'm a cautious person by nature," she added bluntly.

"And I threaten that." He inclined his head once, looking past her for a moment, his eyes veiled behind a screen of impossibly long lashes. Once he had been a master in logistics, mental, physical, emotional. Skilled, accurate, perfect. His trademarks. He had thought that life over. Now, faced with something he wanted very much, he accepted an inescapable truth. No experience was ever truly forgotten no matter how strong the will and the discipline. He focused on her face, seeing the questions in her eyes. Two courses, a frontal assault on the senses or a subtle battle with whatever weapons came to hand. No matter which he chose, there would be only one prize.

Caprice studied him, too conscious of his fingers wrapped around her like a slave bracelet. The urge to pull free was almost overwhelming, but she fought it down. There was no pain or pressure in his grasp, although the promise of both lay subtly in her mind. But overlying all of the caution, the secrets, a strange excitement smoldered. No man had ever had the strength of purpose to pursue her when she had been so blunt. No man had looked at her with such intent. Quin attracted her like fire on a cold night. But like the fire, he spoke silently of destruction, of pain. Neither fit in her plans. Neither would be allowed to blind her to what she sensed in this man with the silver eyes and seldom-seen smile.

"All right," Quin released her wrist. His decision was made. "Have dinner with me, please." This time his words were mild, a polite request for company between two almost strangers.

Caprice's brows arched at the question that made no sense. She started to refuse, the words hovering on the tip of her tongue. But as she opened her mouth to speak she studied him. Suddenly, the hunter was no longer. The danger was gone. The hint of mystery erased. The question dimmed to nothing more than a faint friendliness offered from one person to another. She frowned, unnerved by the change, mistrustful of him and her own senses. "I don't think . . ."

He smiled faintly. "I really like your family. But there is a limit to how much of your puzzling sister, Noelle, I can handle. Besides, as much as I enjoyed the wedding, I don't really want a replay of that either. Take pity on me." He took her hand, tucking it into the crook of his arm in an old-world gesture that conveyed a masculine grace against which Caprice had no defense. He urged her toward the outer door of the restaurant.

Caprice resisted for an instant, logic demanding some kind of reluctance. When he stopped, a polite expression on his face, clearly ready to indulge her, she found it impossible to hold out.

She sensed a trap but could find nothing to support her feelings. Embarrassed, angered at her reaction, she resumed walking. His smile was easy, accepting, and not in the least personal.

"I've never known Noelle to take to anyone the way she did to you. Or Leora either," she added, striving to follow his lead. She'd refuse his invitation in the end, of course, but there was no harm in being pleasant. After all, he had put himself to considerable trouble and expense in having his private plane pick each of them up to bring them to the wedding, as well as seeing to their reservations and arranging the ceremony itself. And he was clearly a friend to Killian and now Silke.

"They are interesting women. A little shy, perhaps, but delightfully unique." He stopped on the sidewalk as the limo that never seemed to be more than a signal away slid noiselessly to a stop beside them. "Shall I promise that I won't make any more remarks to upset you?" He opened the door for her before the driver could. "Will you then change your mind about dinner?"

She searched his face. "You're different," she said, not answering directly.

"I liked what I saw in you. I thought my interest was reciprocated. I was wrong. You told me so. I accept that. End of discussion."

She frowned again, piqued at the quick way he could change his mind. A second later she cursed her own contrariness. She should have been pleased.

"Or course, if you dislike me . . ." Quin looked at her, demanding that reaction if no other.

"No. I don't dislike you. How could I? I don't know you," Caprice said before she thought.

His smile broke. Sunrise after a dark night. Caprice lost her resolve with that smile. No wonder he rarely used it. It was a gesture that warmed without heat, soothed and reassured without a touch, invited without demanding. Her own lips curved.

"All right. Dinner. No more." Besides, like him she had no desire to relive Silke's wedding. All that did was point up the emptiness and the uncertainty of her own life, neither of which she was ready to face.

* * *

Caprice studied her reflection in the mirror. The dress she had chosen was one of the few she had with her and a product of a wardrobe that owed its existence to a woman with little but business on her mind. It wasn't that there was anything wrong with the gown. The simply cut shirtwaist style was elegant, sleek, and clung discreetly in all the right places. The soft gray-green was subtle, not the kind of shade to shout for attention. She had put her hair up in a soft twist. Her jewelry was restrained.

"Boring," she pronounced, glaring at her image. "And why do I care?" She spun away from the mirror, pushing her feet into the high heels she loved but rarely wore because they put her head and shoulders above most men. "But not with Quin." She reached for her handbag just as a light tap sounded on her door.

"You're early," she said quickly as she let Quin in.

He shook back his cuff, consulting his watch.

Caprice inhaled sharply at the scars that ran up his wrist from the back of his hand. "My God. What happened?" she demanded, too stunned by the wanton destruction of something that must have been, at one time, a work of art. Quin was too handsome a man not to have hands to match. She reached out, her fingers lightly tracing the old wounds, feeling the ridges of scar tissue, only guessing at the pain that must have accompanied each raking slash. "That must have been some kind of accident," she whispered, strangely hurt to think of him in pain, damaged, his blood seeping out onto the ground.

Quin studied the soft velvet of her flesh against the bronze of his own. Light and dark. Sun and shadow. He turned his hand in her grasp, taking her palm to the heart of his. "It was a long time ago," he murmured, pleased that she hadn't drawn away from his disfigurement. Some women would have, had in fact. They hadn't hurt him. But she could have.

Caprice looked up, caught by the flash of intensity in his eyes. Before she could fasten on to it, be warned by it, it melted away with his smile.

"I hope you like to dance."

"I do," she answered vaguely, uneasy when she hadn't been a moment before. "Now you see him. Now you don't."

"Riddles?" His light brows lifted curiously as he used the hand he held to pull her gently into the corridor, shutting the door behind him.

"You keep changing on me," she murmured, studying him intently even as she walked beside him to the elevators.

"How?" he asked when the doors slid shut, leaving them alone for the ride down.

She shook her head. "I don't know. I just know that you do. I think you are a dangerous man, Randall Quinlan."

"To you?"

There was just enough amused inquiry in his tone to stiffen Caprice's spine. "Why would I think a man who is only taking me to dinner is dangerous?"

"You brought the idea up. I was only taking it to its natural conclusion."

The elevator opened. Caprice stepped out, too conscious of him beside her. "There is nothing natural about you," she muttered. Too intent on her own reactions, she missed the sudden shift of expression on Quin's face, the sharp look he gave her, and the relaxation of his guard when he realized she didn't know.

"You worry too much, C. R.," he said.

Caprice glanced up, startled by the name that had its roots and use in her professional life. "How did you know about that?"

He tucked her into the limo himself before sliding in beside her. "Your family, remember?"

She grimaced. "I don't want to know what they said."

"Nothing too terrible, I assure you."

"Then you weren't talking to my mother or father."

"That bad?"

She looked away from his face, disturbed by the lightness of his replies. It was almost as though he were going through the motions of the evening, choosing his conversation to convey a certain meaning, a specific image. "Surely, Silke told you about the year all four of us are spending away from home."

Quin leaned back against the cushions, prepared to listen all night if she would talk to him. "We didn't have that much time to get acquainted. And what time we did have was well occupied."

Caprice shot him a sharp look. "Doing what?"

Quin didn't miss a beat. Killian had made it clear that only her parents knew of Silke's covert dealings and that everyone involved wanted the situation to remain under wraps. "Getting engaged and married in less than a week."

She frowned. "I'd believe you if only my sister was involved. She does just about everything at breakneck speed. But Killian doesn't strike me as that kind of man."

"Perhaps a man in love can be forgiven for any number of uncharacteristic behaviors."

"Speaking from experience?"

"No."

Caprice examined the flat reply, finding, oddly, that it asked more than it answered. "Do you believe in love?"

"Do you?"

She shrugged, her gaze holding his in the muted darkness. The words were light. The subject matter controversial enough to intrigue without having any real meaning. Her response should have come easily. "Some kinds of love, yes," she said finally, giving him an honesty and depth that didn't match the tone of the question "Love of parents for children. Children for parents. Puppy love. Sexual love."

"But not the kind that lasts through time and space, lies and truth?" He looked from her face to the scenery passing so silently beyond the dark-tinted windows. Life sped by, a kaleidoscope of energy, dreams, hopes, pain, failures. Love. The greatest and most debilitating emotion of them all. The great equalizer.

"Now you see him. Now you don't."

He turned his head, impaling her with a look. "Is that a wish? Have you changed your mind about me?"

Caprice stilled, her senses alive, alert, on guard. "I don't know what you mean."

The car pulled to a stop. Quin searched her face, feeling her withdrawal as a tangible thing in the silence, an enemy against which he had no weapon beyond the skill and cunning of his own past. "Shall we go in?" He opened the door and slipped out before she answered. He extended his hand.

Caprice studied the elegant, terribly marked fingers. It would have been better if she could have felt some revulsion. Instead, she found she needed to touch him, to soothe that which must have long ago ceased to hurt. She placed her fingers in his. Immediately his strength folded lightly around her hand, cradling rather than imprisoning. He drew her forth from the car.

"Only dinner," she whispered as she stood up beside him.

His eyes glittered in the light of the streetlamps. "As you say. Only dinner."

Quin leaned back against the pillows, staring into the darkness surrounding him. It was well past midnight and his usual time of rest. His life was structured on discipline. He moved through time and space in balance with the energy and forces that flowed around him. Everything had a place, a meaning, a lesson to be taught and learned. He fought no force unseen. Rather he tried to understand, to bend to the seeming whims of creation, whims that were quirks of fate and destiny only to the unenlightened.

Until Caprice. She had bent his structure, forcing him to readjust, realign. The feelings she engendered weren't comfortable, and they certainly weren't emotions with which he was familiar. With another woman, he could have walked away, would have, in fact. But Caprice held a key, although she had no idea of her significance.

Killian had known and remembered, too. Quin had seen that memory in his eyes the night when Silke had mentioned a sister. Quin hadn't been certain until Silke had told him innocently that Caprice was not her genetic sister. That had been the last piece of the puzzle. The forces that had taught him the value of patience, of discipline, of belief in things beyond himself were gathering even now.

Debts. He raised the hands he couldn't see in the darkness. The scars were reminders, although he didn't need them. The prophecy was now.

Three

Caprice stared out the window of the plane, thinking of what she had left behind. Quin. She couldn't forget the name or the man. His impression was stronger than any she had ever known. He called to her in ways she didn't understand, didn't want to understand. From where had the scars come from? The control? Despite the evening they had spent together, she still knew nothing about him. Or almost nothing, she amended silently. One thing she did know was his ability to change before her eyes. It was eerie the way he did a mental and emotional sleight of hand. One moment a hunter, the next a would-be friend. One moment his eyes held knowledge that frightened even as it attracted, and the next only calm inquiry reigned. She shivered faintly, glad she had escaped. He could not know where she was. She hadn't had time to give Silke her address, and she had forgotten to give it to her parents. So she was safe. Startled at the word, the thought, she frowned at the fluffy white clouds she didn't really see. An extreme reaction but she couldn't deny the feeling. Distance from Quin represented safety.

"I've turned into a real coward," she muttered to herself, barely noticing that the plane was gliding in for its landing in Houston.

She deplaned with the rest of the passengers, waited impatiently for her luggage, then headed for the parking lot and her car. Time was running out. The trip to Atlanta had taken longer than she had anticipated. She left the airport, grimacing at the traffic funneling into the city. Houston was her home for the next eleven months, two weeks, and four days. Hell would have been a better name. It wasn't that she didn't like the town. She had nothing against it, except that it wasn't home. Philadelphia and her life were in limbo, and for what? Her mother's whim. One year out of her life. It might as well have been fifty. She had been on the fast track to get somewhere. She had battled the moneyed background that was hers only by adoption. She had fought the image of the daughter hired by the father to a position that stretched her to the limit, and because of what nature had given her, she had fought for respect that didn't come with her blond hair, green eyes, and pin-up proportions.

Her life, thus far, had been one war after another. And now, she had to start over and it just wasn't working. Here, where her mother and father had decreed she begin again, she was a small fish in a large pond. And this fish had no work record, nothing but a degree to set her apart from all those who sought to climb the corporate ladder. So she interviewed, and interviewed, and waited, interviewed again, waited, cursed, interviewed, and waited.

No. No. No. Frustration sat on her shoulder, grinning as the few dollars that she had come to town with dwindled by the hour. Only the fact that she had rented a very low income place in one of the tougher sections of town had given her any margin at all.

Caprice pulled the car into the bare lot that had nothing to recommend it but the numbered slots for each of what were laughingly called apartments. Courtesy of the local thrift shops, she, at least, had furniture . . . of a sort. Opening the door to her cubbyhole, she slung her handbag at the table to the right, kicked off her shoes, and dropped into the overstuffed chair with the faded cushions. It was no beauty, but it was comfortable. Reflexively, she glanced at her watch. One more hour before she had to leave for work. She wondered briefly what her parents would have said if she had told them just what their success-oriented daughter was doing.

"Mother, Father, I'm working in a dive that the locals call Billy's. The only thing it has going for it is that there isn't a topless dancer in sight. The decor is hideous. The clientele is more interested in eyeing the wait staff than the liquor set in front of them. But the tips are good. I eat regularly, and on my days off I hit the interview circuit. Was this what you had in mind for me? Did you honestly think I wouldn't remember what being poor means? That I wouldn't recall hunger and stretching every dime to the length of a dollar?"

She rose and padded to the minuscule bedroom that was just big enough for a full bed and one chest. Thinking about what she had left behind was as useless as her silent conversations. Oddly, she did understand what her parents were trying to do, and for that she had Silke to thank. For a second, a smile curved her lips as she thought of her sister. Who would have guessed that Silke really hadn't been one-tenth the party girl she had always seemed? She, who loved her sister dearly, hadn't seen the strength in Silke, hadn't even considered that there might be more to her than fluff. That fact, combined with the questions Silke had thrown at her that last night, questions about her nonexistent personal life, had pointed fingers at her own tunnel-visioned world. A narrow-range coward. That was her. Quin. His name drifted in and was just as swiftly banished. She had made her decision and she would hold to it. She had much more important things to deal with than one supremely confident man.

Stripping out of her clothes, she slipped into the jeans and top she would wear to the bar. She'd change into her uniform in a scruffy little back room with only a nail on which to hang her own things. Then she'd work a nine-hour shift for a buck an hour plus tips. Hers were good, sometimes too good, causing jealousy among the other girls. They'd tried to cut her out in the beginning, had even gotten away with it for two whole days before her temper had surfaced. From then on, most of them left her alone. Not the most perfect of arrangements because it also meant that when she got in the weeds, which happened even to the best of waitresses, no one would lift a finger to help her get caught up. Caprice shrugged. It wouldn't be forever, she promised herself as she left the apartment and descended three flights of stairs to the street. Before her stint in Houston was over, she would get a job that matched her education. In the meantime, she'd eat and plan and interview.

Quin glanced around the hotel room, nodding in satisfaction. At least this suite had furniture, unlike Killian's apartment. He flipped open his suitcase to put away his clothes. Although a maid went with the suite, he preferred doing his own unpacking. There were certain things in his luggage no one but he and a few of his most trusted staff ever handled. Old habits died hard if at all. He had traveled too much for it to take him too long to finish the chore. When he was done, he sat down at the desk in the sitting room and picked up the phone. It took a little over an hour for him to contact his second in command for an update on his business dealings, a report on Killian and Silke's stay on the island, and finally, a rundown on one Caprice Dayton-St. James.

When he hung up the phone, he had an address and a phone number. There was nothing about a job of any kind and that surprised him considering the conversation they had shared over dinner two nights before. The lady was definitely determined to make her mark on the business world, regardless of her background. He understood the driving need to succeed even if he didn't adhere to it himself. Money interested him only in its barter value. He had no desire to be a Midas hoarding his gold, although he had a considerable amount at present count. Nor did he need his wealth to define his power. He was better acquainted with that than even his most trusted friend or worst enemy. As for success? That, too, had come to him but not because of his own focus on the goal. Rather it was an outgrowth of being a man skilled in an area that few dared, of having the nerve to risk his life and all that he valued on his own strength and commitment to a cause. He and Caprice had a lot in common even if their goals were different. Not that she saw that.

He stared at the address in front of him, planning his next move. So far he had upset her, confused her, and in general mismanaged his whole campaign, something he rarely did. Anger at his own clumsiness was too easy. He slammed the door on the emotion and concentrated on his logic and ability to read others. He had begun to find the keys to Caprice's Pandora's box of motivations. Once he had them all he would know what guise to take to draw her to him. He frowned at the thought.

The prophecy had been clear. For years he had carried it with him, not thinking of it every day but very aware it existed. The gypsy's words had been simple.

"A sister but not a sister. A warrior maid to battle the dark, to tame the dragon and drink from the cup of life."

He had thought he understood and waited for the warrior maid. Then he had found her when he was least expecting her. He had given her honesty that he had given no other, for he had learned that honesty in the wrong hands was a sword of death. In return she had given him fear. That had hurt, confused him for a moment, made him doubt his assessment and the words of the seer. That fear had also forced him to wrap himself in one of his many disguises. He had hated the necessity. If she were the one for whom he had waited all these years, she deserved more and better of him than what he had given so many others.

Caprice stretched tiredly, rubbing the base of her spine to ease out the kinks of working a double shift. The level of noise in the bar seemed higher than usual. Certainly the customers had been more rambunctious in the week she had been back from Atlanta. She would definitely have a few bruises tomorrow from the lecherous hands she hadn't been able to elude.

"You all right, honey?" Belle muttered as she leaned against the bar beside Caprice.

Caprice started, surprised at the comment that sounded sincere from the ringleader of those who ignored her. "Yes, thanks," she said finally, looking at the older woman. Perpetual weariness darkened Belle's eyes, adding years to her age.

"You did Rose a good turn," she explained awkwardly. "Bubba would have fired her if you hadn't gone to bat for her and agreed to take her shift as well."

Caprice shrugged, not even certain herself why she had pushed to help the younger girl who had never had a kind word for her. "She has a child and no husband," she murmured.

Belle's brows rose. "She told you?"

"I heard you talking."

Belle shifted restlessly, really looking at the woman they had all done their best to alienate. She didn't fit in, and they all knew it. For one thing, her language set her apart. But she did her work and she didn't steal tips from the rest of them. "Maybe we were wrong," she said at last, her gaze sliding away, then back. "We thought you were just slumming. Figured we'd have to carry you." She spread her hands helplessly. "This ain't much, but for most of us it's all we got."

Caprice nodded. She remembered the feeling too well for comfort. "I would have probably done the same."

Belle's expression lightened. "You mean that? You won't hold it against us?"

Caprice shook her head. "No."

Belle sighed deeply, then grinned slightly. "You wanna come with us to the pizza place tomorrow night, after we get off?"

Caprice recognized the olive branch. She had nothing in common with these women who counted their lives in dollars scrimped and saved. But to refuse would hurt them much more than herself. "I'd like that."

"It's Dutch."

Laughing, Caprice picked up her tray. "Is there any other way?"

Belle chuckled. "You're all right, St. James," she replied, tucking her own tray against her well-rounded hip. She cast a look over the crowded bar, suddenly frowning. She caught Caprice's arm when she would have moved away. "See that guy over there? The one who just sat down in your station?"

Caprice followed her look, then nodded. The man was burly, bearded, and looked mean enough to go a round or two with a bear and win. "What about him?"

"He ain't nice at all. Watch his hands, especially if he drops something on the floor in front of you. Don't reach down for it. No matter what he says."

Caprice looked back at Belle's face, seeing the sincerity in her eyes. "I can handle it."

"You could if he wasn't Bubba's cousin. He thinks it gives him rights to the help, and you're new talent."

Caprice glanced back at the man, feeling the anger build. She was thirty and had had more than her share of passes. And if the worst happened, she could walk away from this job and never look back. It would mean she would have to cry uncle, but there were worse things, things such as Belle was implying. Sexual harassment and humiliation. Male bullying. Anger built, her eyes flashing a warning that even Belle could see.

"Honey, don't do it. Bubba'll have you outta here before you can say spit. And he won't be nice about it either, and he sure won't care who's listening." Belle looked past Caprice to the table and its impatient customer. "Let me get him for you. He won't bother me."

Caprice shook her head. "My customer. My problem."

"Ain't yours, honey. That S.O.B. would have been Rose's, and she's my best friend."

Caprice's eyes narrowed, thinking of Rose, the slender blonde with the sad eyes and the little girl without a father. "How long has he been hitting on Rose?"

Belle looked away, shrugging uncomfortably. "Don't know."

She did know, Caprice decided. Too much. And she needed her job as much as Rose did. "Like I said, my customer." She settled her tray on her hip, not even noticing the brevity of her costume with its French maid black skirt, fishnet stockings, and halter cut-to-China top. Bubba didn't like his girls to tie their hair back, so hers swung loose in a silver cloud down her back, its ends stopping an inch short of the minuscule skirt hem.

Belle's face creased with anxiety. "Stay out of his range, Caprice. No matter what he does, don't get within grabbing range."

Caprice hardly heard her. Her gaze was focused on the man who had evidently been terrorizing the rest of the women. She wasn't them, and she damn well didn't believe that any man had the right to force himself on a woman, be it mentally or physically. Swaying between tables, she bore down on her quarry.

Quin glared at the seedy-looking establishment squatted against the sidewalk in front of him. A neon sign with one *L* unlit proclaimed Billy's in bright pink and orange. The combination was as tasteless as the music spilling out of its open door to pollute the night.

"This can't be right. There is no way Caprice is working in a place like this. I'm on a damn wild goose hunt."

He got out of the rented Mercedes, glared at the dimly lit street. He'd be lucky if the car wasn't stripped before he got back. The only thing making him follow this lead through to its conclusion was the fact that the phone company had been very specific about the first name on its billing. There couldn't be that many Caprice St. Jameses getting a new phone in Houston in the same week. And the woman at the tacky apartment complex had been even more specific in describing the C. R. St. James who lived on the third floor. Quin slammed his car door and strode across the street. Smoke swirled around him as he entered the dim room. The wall of sound was even more off-putting on closer acquaintance.

"Listen up, girlie, you made me drop it. You'll pick it up."

The nasty edge to the rough voice caught Quin's attention as he stood in the doorway, surveying the room. He followed the sound to the corner table. The flash of silver hair on the waitress with her back to him trapped his glance. Caprice. There could be no other woman with that kind of figure and that shade of moonlight hair. He took a step closer just as the heavyset man with the ugly mouth reached out a beefy hand and wrapped it around Caprice's waist. Rage erupted in Quin's eyes at the sight of that filthy hand on Caprice's soft body. Quin didn't waste time with the curse in his mind. He cleared the three tables around him in two steps, wading through the ring forming to watch the confrontation. Just as he reached Caprice, she twisted to her right, out of the man's hold, brought her tray down on his balding head with a thump, and then followed that up with a spike heel jammed into his instep.

Her attacker let out a howl that sounded like a raging bull and shot to his feet, murder in his eyes.

Quin stepped between Caprice and the man, shielding her even as he faced the bully. His opponent stopped in his tracks, his eyes bulging at the giant who could have frozen hell itself with his eyes.

"Ain't your fight," he muttered balefully, his fists swinging meaningfully.

Quin balanced on the balls of his feet, waiting. The eyes, not blustery words, would tell him when his man would make his move. "I'm making it mine. You've got the manners of an ass with no training. The lady didn't deserve it. No woman does."

"She ain't no lady. None of these women are," he sneered, glancing around, his eyes finding each of the waitresses as though he knew exactly where they were.

Quin read the look and the man, even as he ignored Caprice's outraged hiss. His glance never wavered from his target as he absorbed and cataloged the full character of the male specimen before him. "Are you going to run your mouth or prove you're more than a bully with someone weaker and smaller than you? Or don't you have the guts?" Each question was a soft, almost gentle inquiry. Around them, the noise abated, the eye of a hurricane in full fury.

Bubba's cousin shifted angrily, judging his man. "I ain't got no fight with you."

"You do. She belongs to me."

He absorbed that, rage spitting from the look he slashed at Caprice. "She didn't say nothin'."

Quin waited.

He looked back at Quin, fighting the need to show off and knowing he'd lose if he tried. Before he could speak, Bubba came rushing into the center of the circle.

"What's going on here?" he demanded, out of breath.

Quin sliced him a glare. "What's going on is this creep is harassing your waitresses. He has the interesting opinion that this is a pit stop for hookers and he only has to pick out his model."

Bubba drew himself up, trying to stretch his inches to match Quin's. It was a useless exercise at best. "I haven't seen you in here before."

Quin didn't bother with a reply. He turned to Caprice. The second his back was angled away from Caprice's tormentor, he struck.

Or tried to. The blow never landed. In a smooth move, learned
long before Quin had learned to shave, Quin flowed around, his
hands and feet shifting in a maneuver so effortless that it looked
unreal. It ended with a soft series of thuds, and then his opponent
lay on the floor at Quin's feet, his hands pressed to his stomach
and knee, groaning as though in terrible pain. Quin looked at him
for a moment, then raised his eyes to Bubba.

"I didn't break anything but I should have."

Bubba swallowed noisily as he backed up three steps. His eyes
fell on Caprice as she stood as transfixed as everyone else at what
Quin had done. "You're fired," he breathed hoarsely.

"Wrong," Quin spoke gently. "She quits." He slipped the bow
lose that held her apron, dipped his hands in the twin pockets, and
took out the tips filling the cavities. Dropping change and bills in
his jacket pocket, he pulled the tray from her grasp and tossed it
on the table. "Have you got any clothes of your own or is this
yours?" he asked in that same gentle tone that made ice seem hot.

Caprice stared at him, seeing the perfectly controlled rage
clouding his eyes. "In the back."

He nodded once. "Go change. I'll wait." He looked beyond her
to the crowd. At once, the circle split, clearing an aisle for Caprice.

Caprice wanted to argue, but something, some sense of gratitude
and a healthy dose of self-preservation, made her dam her words
unspoken and do exactly as he said. It only took a few minutes for
her to put on her jeans and top and leave the uniform in the changing
stall. Belle was poised at the entrance when she walked out.

"He told me to stay right here until you were done. He don't
trust that Bubba." She patted Caprice's arm. "You did good, honey.
Don't think that creep will be hitting on any of us anytime soon.
You tell your man we said thanks a heap."

Caprice nodde,d not sure she could explain to Belle exactly
what Quin was even if she had the time. She didn't know herself.

Four

"I wish you would just say something," Caprice said finally.
They had been in the car for at least five of the longest minutes
of her life and Quin had yet to speak.

Quin glanced at her, measuring her defensive position as she sat slightly at an angle, her back to the passenger door. "What would you like me to say?"

She stared at him. The voice was as calm as if they were discussing the weather rather than the fact that he had just rescued her from a potential barroom brawl. Add to that he had seen her clobber a man with a tray and, in general, act like a woman of the streets rather than one of the heirs to the St. James's fortune. "I expected a lecture at least," she said finally, honestly.

He shrugged and returned his attention to the traffic. "Not my right."

That stopped her, but only for a moment. "You don't have any questions either?"

"You're over twenty-one. If you chose a dive for a place to work, I have to assume you wanted the job there."

Caprice thought that over and found she didn't like either his attitude or his answers. "I didn't want the job. It was the only one I could get."

"Competition." He inclined his head. "I can understand that. I'm just surprised that your experience with St. James Inc. didn't have more clout." He made the last turn to her apartment, pulling into the slot beside her car.

Caprice was startled to discover she hadn't even given a thought to the fact that she had left the vehicle at the bar. "How did that get here?"

"I had it driven here."

"Why?"

"Your vanquished opponent might have let his beer courage get past his instinct for survival. I'm really not in the mood to deal with the police and the legal system." He got out of the car and came around to her side before she could open the door herself. He extended his hand.

Caprice put her own in his before she could think of a good reason not to. "I didn't thank you for coming to my rescue. I don't think Bubba would have done a thing if his cousin had knocked me through the wall."

Quin tucked her hand in the crook of his arm. "Probably not," he agreed.

Caprice glanced at him, trying to decide exactly where she was in the conversation. Nothing about Quin indicated any anger, but she felt something so akin to the rage she had seen in his eyes that she doubted her own senses. His voice was smooth, dark as the night around them, almost gentle. But it was the kind of gentleness that beguiled as it wrapped its words in secrets. "You don't have to come in with me."

"Have you had dinner yet?" He didn't pause as they reached the second landing, but continued to climb steadily. Every step was one piece of a pattern, a calming rhythm like the actions of maneuvering the car through the city streets. He had used those moments as he was using these to come down from the mountain of his own fury.

"No," Caprice murmured, stopping in front of her door.

"How long will it take you to change?"

"You don't have to feed me."

"I want to." He took the key from her hand and unlocked her door himself, then urged her before him into the small apartment. He looked around, missing nothing, not the threadbare, used furniture, the single telephone, the tiny rooms, or the lack of amenities.

Caprice could imagine how her place to sleep looked through his eyes. Nothing short of a complete renovation would have improved it. She waited for him to say something, but she waited in vain. He simply walked across the room and settled into the only chair large enough to hold him. He gazed at her, his brows arched.

"You do silence very well," she said with a snap, her own anger getting the better of her. "I know it isn't much."

"I think it's perfect," he disagreed.

She blinked, stunned enough at his comment to swallow the rest of her explanation.

"You were in a temper when you picked this place out. This is the second time I've seen you impulsive, out of control. Like tonight. That bully made you mad. So you got even." He shrugged, smiling faintly. For the first time since he had seen the fear in her eyes, there was hope.

"That doesn't sound nice."

"Nice is boring. Ordinary. Human pap for the apathetic."

She laughed shortly l amused and a little unnerved at the assessment. "That's direct enough."

"A lie would be better?"

She turned from him and dropped her handbag on the table beside the door. "No. Just easier to deal with." She glanced over her shoulder, for one second looking into those eyes that could change so swiftly that a blink was slow in comparison. "You confuse me."

"I know."

"I think you do it on purpose."

He said nothing.

"No denial?"

"You stated an opinion, not a fact."

"That's no answer."

"It's all I have right now."

She frowned, wanting to demand answers and equally afraid of what she would hear.

Quin nodded toward the bedroom. "Go change. I'm not going anywhere tonight."

Caprice went. Valor bowed to discretion, then retired from the field.

Quin watched her go, his mind working at top speed. That bully didn't know it, but he had done Quin a favor. Caprice was off balance now. The fear was there but not triggered yet, rather lying in wait. This time he was prepared. He glanced down at his hands, allowing them to curl into the fists that matched the rage still seething inside. Caprice didn't realize it, but right now she was safer with him than she ever had been. Too much emotion was roiling within him. To control it, he had to shut down. He had to deal only on the most superficial levels until he could forget the image of that cruel grip that would have wounded, damaged, and humiliated for the sake of primitive lust. Images of the past superimposed themselves on the present. He had seen worse. He had also avenged worse with a heavier hand than he had used tonight. That was one of his dragons, his shadow demons that could not be defeated, his darkness that could not be lit but by one candle.

He looked up, hearing the sounds of water running. For one moment, he let go of his will and allowed his imagination to feed his emptiness, to bring alive the future for which he had waited all these years. Caprice. A shower. Slender curves glistening with moisture and tiny soap bubbles. She would be pink, mauve, and cream. Warmth and satiny skin to wrap around his body. Her scent would be woman, ready and waiting to mate. Her eyes would glitter with her need and the excitement of the ritual. He would touch her. So gently. He knew how. The nerves that gave pleasure without end. The muscles that could shift and ripple with such power that no movement would be wasted. He was a skilled lover, well versed in techniques that had begun in societies that specialized in sensual delight. He would bring those gifts to her, lay them at her feet for her joy, her fulfillment. His warrior maid. He now knew the prophecy had not lied.

Caprice dressed quickly, conscious of the minutes ticking away and Quin settled so silently in her living room. She had thought to escape him. She had been wrong. When she had looked up and seen him step between her and certain injury tonight, she had discovered that she was worried about him, worried with a depth that didn't match the nearly stranger status. Then she had watched him take over, somehow directing everyone, her tormentor, herself, Bubba, even the crowd. He had claimed her, and she had done little to stop him, at that second hadn't even wanted to. Then he had turned his back on his opponent. She had barely registered the other man's intentions when Quin had moved, sliding into a stance that was familiar and yet subtly different from any defensive maneuver she had ever seen or heard about. His hands and feet had been silent, accurate weapons. But his eyes had held the key to all that he did. He had known just how hard to hit and where. He had known exactly the moment when that cowardly hand would connect. He had known where she and everyone around them were. And when it was over, he had looked at her, his gaze searching for damage, promising retribution if he found any. Then he had looked past her to the crowd, and they had mutely stepped aside as though he had roared a command. No hand had been lifted against them as they had left. No voice had shouted insults or demanded a rematch. No one had dared.

Danger. Tonight her friend. A tame lion to stroll at her side, to protect her from all who would threaten her. She smiled faintly at the image. Until this second, it had not occurred to her that Quin could be tamed by any hand. Suddenly, the fear that had driven her from Atlanta, that had dogged her thoughts, that demanded her caution seemed foolish, a product of her own narrow life. She rose and slipped her feet into another pair of high heels to match the discreet black dress that was one of her favorites. Unlike the last meal they had shared, this one would happen as it willed, she decided. Whatever Quin was, she would discover the spectrum of the man. Maybe she wouldn't like what she found, but she was through running.

"I'm ready," she announced as she entered the living room to find him looking out the single window that overlooked the parking lot.

Quin turned, barely noticing the body that he had imagined. Her expression was his goal. The clear light in her eyes surprised him as much as it pleased him. She was not afraid. She was interested, perhaps even intrigued. A good beginning.

"Do you like steak?" He came to her and took her hand.

The gesture was always there, a strange courtesy in this modern day and yet it somehow fit the man. "The kind with lots of mushrooms?"

He smiled. "If you like."

His smile touched her, soothing, inviting her to relax with him. An hour before her decision she wouldn't have been able to accept the invitation. Her lips curved as she inclined her head. Once more she was aware of the strength and size of him as he dwarfed her even in the heels. "Lead me to it. Considering I'm now unemployed, I'd better have a good last meal."

Quin's smile widened into a grin. She was coming to hand, delicately but definitely. He had not hoped for so much so soon. "You don't sound too upset about the situation." He locked the door behind them and checked it carefully.

"I'm not. I was just about ready to decide I wasn't tough enough anymore for that kind of job."

"As you once were?" His brows lifted, trying to imagine her permanently in the setting in which he had found her. The image wouldn't come. She was made for more.

She laughed softly. "You sound as if you don't know about me."

"I know that you were adopted." Actually, he could have known everything up to and including her bra size, but he had hated the thought of investigating her or pumping Killian for answers. He would have resented anyone digging into his own background, invading his privacy.

"I'm surprised Silke didn't tell you. It's hardly a secret after all."

They reached the ground floor. Quin pushed open the door and ushered her outside. In her climb to reach the top, Caprice had lost, if she had ever had, the need to be taken care of by a man. And when a few had tried, they had handled the gestures, the words so badly that she had felt demeaned as a woman to the point that she had refused any and all attempts at those kinds of courtesies later. Yet Quin made his care of her so natural, so much a part of his own nature, that she discovered a kind of warmth that had never been. He made her feel special. It was that simple. He made her feel as though he were truly glad to have her company. Once again, he had shown her another facet of himself. First, the man bent on having her. Then the impersonal stranger, and now someone who wanted to share with her. Even his questions added to that impression, curious, probing lightly, but with very real interest. Had she found the real man at last? she wondered as she watched him walk around the front of the car and slide behind the steering wheel.

"Silke didn't have time to tell me much of anything at all. As I told you, she and Killian were very involved in tying up some loose ends," Quin murmured, picking up the conversation without missing a beat.

"You never did explain what you were doing in Atlanta. I heard Killian say something about your having been there for a little more than a week."

"I do a lot of traveling. I ended up in the right place at the right time." He started the car.

"Is that how you also ended up arranging the wedding?"

"I was the only one with free time. Both Killian and Silke were involved with their jobs and setting up their replacements as well as trying to close up both apartments, get blood tests and a marriage license. I had some free time, so I offered to help."

"That covers you. What about Killian? What was he doing in Atlanta in the first place? Although I hadn't met him until the wedding, his company and my father's have been doing business for years. I hardly think he needs to go hunting for work."

"He was helping out a friend."

"Was that part of the unfinished business?" Caprice asked curiously.

"Partially."

"You aren't going to tell me anything else, are you?"

He shook his head. "Not my story. Ask Killian if you want to know that much."

"You have very definite ideas on what is private, don't you?"

He glanced at her briefly. "You think that's odd?"

"I come from a world where almost everything has a price and there are few secrets, even among friends."

He shrugged faintly, his shoulders rippling with the move. "That's true in most places, with most people. But there is always an exception or two. The trick is to make sure you know who you're trusting."

"The voice of experience." Her comment was automatic, and she vaguely expected the same in return. What she got was silence, short but very definite.

"Yes," he said finally. He pulled into the parking lot of the restaurant he had chosen, shut off the motor, and angled his body toward her so that he could monitor her reactions. "Do you really want to know about me, or is it just idle conversation?"

Caprice blinked, not having expected the blunt question. He was nothing like any man she had ever known. "Are you always this direct?"

"That's no answer."

She spread her hands, uneasy again, pressed into a corner that had nothing to do with physical strength. "How do I answer a question like that?"

"The same way it was asked. Honestly."

"Then I hand you more leverage than maybe I want to deal with right now."

His eyes narrowed. "Still running?"

"I don't know what you mean."

"You know, all right," he returned in a low growl of building anger. "Do you really want me to play games with you? I can. Better probably than you can even imagine. I thought you had more sense, more honesty than that."

"You don't know me."

"Don't I?" He wrapped his long fingers around her shoulders, making no move to draw her close but implying that the possibility would exist until he decided to let her go. "I know that you're smart, too smart in some ways. I know you need to have your feet firmly on what you consider stable ground. I know you don't take chances of any kind. And I know you are here, doing something so different from your real life that only some very powerful force, more perhaps than the love you have for your adoptive parents, could have commanded the change. I also know you don't like being here. And that you can lose your temper and, when you do, you'll charge hell with a bucket of sand if the whim takes you. I know you care about your family and your sisters, but you aren't really a part of them. And I know you want me, but you would cut out your own tongue before you would say so."

Caprice stared at him, stunned at the anger driving each of his words as well as the accuracy with which he had read her. She felt stripped, vulnerable, open to attack, under siege. "Stop it," she whispered, wrapping her hands around his wrists to free herself. But no matter how much she pulled and pushed, she didn't gain an inch of freedom. Panting, fear licking at her thoughts, she finally stopped fighting. She glared at him in the semidarkness, her eyes glittering with fury. "You spoke of rights. Will you steal mine, now? Will you use your strength to break me?" she demanded. "I trusted you."

"Did you, Caprice? Or did you decide to do a little testing of the waters before you put your toe in to swim?" Still he made no move to draw her close, although he easily could have. Desire was a caged beast, growling, flexing its muscles in anticipation of its own feeding.

"What do you want from me?" she breathed, staring into his light eyes, seeing cloudy, miniature reflections of her own imprisoned self.

"I told you once that I would give you anything you asked of me but my absence. Do you remember?"

She nodded slowly.

"I will answer you, but first, tell me which way you want it. A stupid game that strangers play to decide if they want to bed one another or the truth?"

All of her life, Caprice had prized the truth. She had been lied to too many times by her mother and her "fathers" and "uncles" to accept anything less. She had also demanded the right to choose for herself her own destiny. Only with this move to Houston had she bowed to another's will. Yet, faced with the choice that Quin laid before her, a choice that incorporated two of her most valuable beliefs, she discovered that she had only been fooling herself all these years. She didn't want to pick one answer. She didn't want the responsibility. Quin was right. She had come tonight, testing the waters, ready to let the choice of what would happen between them lie more with him than with her. In that moment, she faced herself with a clearer vision than ever before.

"The truth," she whispered, her fingers unknowingly holding on to his wrists for support rather than freedom.

Quin searched her eyes, seeing the fear and the courage. The warrior maid was learning her strength. "I want you. Any way that I can have you now."

"And lat . . ." Before she could finish the word he shook his head.

"Let that be enough for tonight. Don't ask me more than you're ready to hear." He pulled her slowly toward him, giving her time to protest, to resist.

Caprice surrendered to the pressure of his hands, not sure what waited for her in his arms, but knowing she intended to find out. Power wrapped around her. An elemental force that could chain or enchant at will.

He folded her close to his chest, tucking her head against his shoulder, her body molded to his. Her scent was an invisible web to trap his senses, whispering silently of what would come. Desire growled deeply, demanding release that wasn't granted. Patience had never been harder. Need never stronger. Determination never greater. He held her, absorbing her softness, her light. She had given. He had frightened her, but she had come to him even though he had offered her an escape.

"Thank you."

Caprice heard the words as they rumbled deeply from his chest. She lifted her head, her eyes wide with shock. "For what?"

He touched her face, tracing the delicate line of her jaw, the faint jut of her chin, the elegant curve of her brow. "For not asking for the game. I would have played it for you, but it would have hurt."

Caprice looked into his eyes, seeing the shadows he made no attempt to conceal. He was vulnerable. The knowledge passed through her, mental lightning to light up her emotions. She cupped his face, her fingers splayed from chin to ear. His skin was warm, faintly rough from his beard. "How would it have hurt?" she asked softly, feeling as though she was treading ground untouched by any other woman. Virgin territory.

"For every lie one lives, a piece of one's self is offered to fate. Enough lies and nothing is left to give to another."

"But you would have done it for me?"

His gaze holding hers, he turned his lips to the palm of her hand, his kiss a caress that promised but didn't brand. "Yes." He saw the why forming on her lips, the question that neither of them was prepared to face. He leaned forward, stealing the question, offering her his mouth. Her sigh was gentle, intriguing, a feminine plea that reached past the beast of desire to the lamb of tenderness.

Caprice relaxed in his arms, no longer wanting words to fill the silence when his fire warmed it so very well. Her arms encircled his neck, drawing him nearer still. His taste was as unique as the man, spicy, exotic, intoxicating. She moaned softly as his tongue claimed her, teaching her his art of oral lovemaking. Parry, retreat, thrust. Her need rose, teased by each foray. Then soothed with the touch of his hands sweeping in long strokes down her back, probing a web of nerves at the base of her spine. She arched, strangely energized, her flesh tingling, heat flashing beneath her skin, sizzling in streaks of fire to the farthest reaches of her limbs.

"Quin," she breathed hoarsely, her eyes opening despite the great weights that seemed attached to her lashes. "Please."

He lifted his head, his nostrils flaring to catch each nuance of her scent, the changes that ebbed and flowed with the desire growing even now in the silence. "I will please you, I promise," he murmured. "But for now, only a little." He nipped lightly at the pulse beating at the base of her throat. "We must know each other better first."

Caprice threaded her fingers through his hair, holding him to her, wanting his kiss as she had wanted few things in her life. "I know enough."

He traced the outline of the bodice of her dress, his fingers dipping ever so slightly beneath the fabric to tease the flesh he could have claimed as his own. "A little," he corrected roughly. He raised his eyes to hers, demanding she see what he could have hidden. "When you aren't afraid to ask and I'm not afraid to answer then we will reach for this and take all the pleasure that it holds."

Five

He spoke not of if but of when, for himself and for her. Caprice faced him in the darkness, close enough to hear his heartbeat, to read every change of expression. "So certain?"

"You aren't?"

"I shouldn't be."

He set her gently from him. "Will you come with me?"

She looked beyond him to the restaurant. "Yes. I think I must if I am to have any peace with myself." She glanced back to him.

His smile touched her, holding the same kind of inevitability that lived in her voice. Without a word, he got out of the car and came around to her side, opened her door, and offered her his hand. "Then come with me and we will speak of things past and present."

"No future?"

He tucked her hand in the crook of his arm. "Not tonight."

The evening progressed just as he had promised. Caprice found herself telling him of her adoption and even a little of the years before. His questions, when they came, were thoughtful, compassionate, and intelligent. She didn't have to guard her words or search for hidden meanings. But more than that, his man bore no resemblance to the impersonal one who had dined with her a few days ago. This Quin smiled, not often but enough to let her know that he found pleasure in her company.

"So tell me about yourself," she invited over dessert.

"Like you, I have no birth people of my own. I knew my mother, once, a long time ago. My father died when I was less than two." He lifted his snifter of brandy, swirling the liquor gently in the bulb glass before taking a sip. "I am part American and the rest is Tzigane."

"As in gypsy?"

He nodded, waiting for the kinds of questions his background always seemed to bring to the fore.

Caprice caught his reaction, the faint tensing of his muscles. She was beginning to know this man. She could only guess at some of the inane things about his heritage he must have heard through the years. "I know very little about the life. Will you tell me?"

Quin released his tension with a faint sigh. Always the unexpected with Caprice. "There aren't as many of us as there once were. Perhaps we are an endangered species." He looked past her into his own history. "I was born in Europe, caught in the mountains, halfway between two countries that don't exist anymore. My father delivered me and the sister who came after me."

"You're a twin?"

He shook his head. "No. She was born a year later, only then there was no storm coming, no wind screaming down the mountain like a woman in labor. Spring had touched the day she entered the world. But winter had a stranglehold on the night she left it."

Caprice inhaled sharply when she suddenly realized that his poetic phrasing spoke of death. "How old was she?"

"Twelve." He took a deep swallow of his brandy.

"An accident?"

He shook his head, his expression scarred with the memories of his sister. "Her death was no accident," he said flatly.

"Murder?" Caprice searched his face, seeing the hurt and the rage that the passage of time had not dimmed.

He finished the last of his drink and set the glass aside. He wasn't ready to answer that question, so he ignored it. "We lived in a caravan until that winter, traveling between countries as though no borders existed. A Tzigane needs the freedom of open spaces, of sky without end. It is their breath and life. Chain the Tzigane and you hold a rabid human wolf who only bows to power greater than his own long enough to accomplish his freedom or his death."

Caught by the strange phrasing, the story unfolding, Caprice discovered yet more facets of the man called Quin. He had the soul of a poet, the eyes of a cynic, and the words of a realist. And memories that held a darkness to match her own. For the first time since she had met Quin, she felt as though they might have something in common.

"You sound as though you felt the weight of that kind of chain."

He focused on her face, finding a soft light in eyes he had seen in so many moods. "I did," he said simply.

"Were you a rabid wolf?"

"No, only a well-trained hunter."

She frowned at the reply that left no room for doubt. "I don't understand."

"The country we were in was military ruled. I committed a crime in their eyes, so I was taken away from my family. I never saw them again."

Appalled, Caprice stared at him. He stated the facts with such an absence of emotion that it took a moment for the ramifications to set in. "What kind of crime?"

He watched her eyes, dissecting every change of expression. He had spent his life taking risks. He knew no other way to live, wanted no other way. But she was different than he. She needed security, the kind of safety he would never be able to offer her. There was just too much that had gone before, too much that couldn't be undone even if he regretted it enough to try.

"I killed the men who stole my sister's life."

Caprice looked for shock within herself and found only acceptance. Some part of her had known he had avenged his sister. He was a man who would always fight for and protect those who mattered to him. She had seen it in the bar, when he had stepped between her and injury. But in spite of that knowledge, the age factor made the choice exceptional. "You were only thirteen."

Quin exhaled softly, tension easing from his body. He had known he would tell her of this, the beginning of his life. He wanted her more with every moment he spent with her, but he would not take her as his mate if she did not know what manner of man held her in his arms, what hands gave her pleasure to light the night, what voice whispered of dark, delicious secrets that only lovers share. "In my world, a man. It was enough."

"They caught you, didn't they?"

He nodded. "And put me in a cage."

"You escaped?"

"No." His lips twisted into a grim curve, his eyes dark with memories that he would never share. "I was offered my freedom. I took the deal."

Caprice examined the idea and found it strange. "What kind of deal?"

"The men I had killed were soldiers. My methods were better than theirs. Their superior was impressed. He offered to clear the charges if I would submit to training with his group."

"You agreed?"

"Tziganes care little for politics. And I didn't condemn the group for the sake of a few. I had learned that from my mother's knee. The murderers were dead. And that man held the key to the cage. It seemed a fair exchange."

Caprice understood choices made out of necessity. She had made a number of those herself. "Is that when you became a hunter?"

"Yes." He looked away from her to signal for the check.

"Are you still?" she murmured, understanding now how and why he had handled Bubba's cousin so easily.

He faced her again. "No. I found I no longer had any taste for the life."

"What do you do?"

"Solve puzzles?"

"What kind of puzzles?"

Quin paused only long enough to hand over his gold card when the waiter arrived. "Old ones, most of the time. Bits of history, written in strange tongues by peoples with customs and language patterns different from today."

"No government snooping?"

"Rarely."

"But still some?"

He nodded. "Not much. Computers work very well in that area now." He rose, taking her hand in his. "Were you expecting something more colorful for an ex-soldier gypsy?" he murmured for her ears alone.

"I'm learning not to expect anything where you're concerned," she admitted wryly. "I'm invariably wrong."

"Not comfortable and you like comfort and security." He accepted his credit card and receipt from the waiter, scrawling his name across the bottom of the latter before ushering Caprice out of the restaurant.

"I *need* comfort and security," Caprice corrected honestly. "I spent too many years living hand to mouth, not knowing whether there would be food to eat when I woke up in the morning or even the same room and bed in which I had gone to sleep. I don't remember a year of my early life when I had the same things to play with as I had had the year before. We were always just one step ahead of the bill collectors or some man who thought my mother owed him something. I thought I would forget when Lorraine and Geoffrey adopted me. I had everything I had ever thought was important, but no matter how much I have, I haven't lost that need to count what belongs to me, to hold on, to hoard, to need things more than people." She shrugged awkwardly. "I guess I'm not a nice person.

He stopped beside his car, turning her to face him. The sadness in her eyes hurt, but he didn't let her see that. He concentrated instead on her feelings, her needs. "Do you really want to be something as bland as that?"

She smiled without humor. "Bland or not, I would like to be proud of my value system, feel as though I weren't just amassing money for money's sake, that I wasn't so selfish."

"So change," he challenged her. "Put the past away. Slam the door on it."

She leaned against the car, watching the play of light across his face. "Wave a magic wand and transform myself. Instant nice." This time her smile did hold humor, self-directed and real. "My mother would bow to Mecca for the rest of her life if I did." She reached up, her fingers touching his cheek, the strong line of his jaw. "You're a different kind of man, Randall Quinlan. Strange ideas, perfect-sense kinds of things that real people don't usually have enough courage or strength to do."

He covered her hand with his, pressing it against his skin. She didn't know it, but this was the first touch she had offered him that had nothing to do with passion or wanting. Her eyes were tender, another first, her voice softer than he had yet to hear it. "I think you underestimate yourself. You can do anything if you just believe it's possible." Even before he finished speaking, she was shaking her head.

"In business, probably. In my personal life, I doubt it."

"Doubting is not the same as no." He urged her hand to his lips. He caressed the center of her palm with the tip of his tongue. Her skin had a spicy taste, so like her scent that he felt the effect on two levels. He accepted both but focused on her mind. "You didn't think this was possible. You even ran from it," he reminded her gently.

Caprice shivered faintly at the truth she couldn't deny even had she wanted to. "It's not the same. The lessons aren't as deep or as long-standing."

"Now whose reasons make sense?" He used the hand he held to pull her to his body. He wrapped his arm around her waist, urging her closer so that they rested hip to hip, thigh to thigh. Intimate, a lover's embrace that, despite the clothes holding them chaste, lost none of its power to incite. He inhaled deeply, drawing her into him in the only way the public place would allow. Her touch imprinted itself on his flesh, her scent branded his senses. Her warmth was a soft blanket of life.

"I don't feel sensible," she whispered, relaxing into his strength, no longer afraid of the attraction that held her as securely as any of the chains of which he had spoken.

"No, you feel soft and infinitely desirable." Quin traced her lips with his forefinger. "And very kissable."

Caprice brushed the tip of his finger with her kiss, her eyes holding his. She watched the desire smoldering there flare. Feminine satisfaction and pride at her power over him were swift, telling. In his arms, she felt more of a woman than she had ever thought she could be. "You talk too much."

"Only because not talking will get us both arrested," he murmured, bending his head to accept the kiss she held waiting. Her mouth was all that he remembered, beguilingly sweet and hot. She took but gave as well. He felt her fingers curl like claws into his jacket, her mark for her man. Desire slipped loose one link of the chain that held it tame. He caught her hands, tucking them into his and holding them against his chest. To control himself, he first had to control her.

"We can't catch fire here," he breathed roughly as he raised his head to search her eyes. The passion he found in the glittering depths matched his own hunger. "Will you have me tonight? Will you trust me that much? Give yourself to me?"

"I wish you hadn't asked. It would be so much easier if you just let it happen."

"Not easy." He cupped her chin, outlining the stubborn tilt. "We are not easy people. And I don't want you to come to me driven by need without thought. I don't just want your body, passionate though it is."

"Love me for my mind," she tried to joke. To take him seriously brought back the fear, the need to run away.

"Don't," he commanded, suddenly angry.

"I have to. Don't you see?" The plea emerged before she could stop it.

Quin shook off the excuse and went for the heart of the reality. "I see you running again."

"I want you. I'm not running from that."

"No, you're definitely not," he agreed, releasing her chin to slide his hand down her side to the joining of their bodies. "So you want the game after all. The test drive for the relationship. 'Good in bed and maybe I'll let him know me. Then again maybe I will not.'" His glance flashed with anger and frustration. "Are those not the rules?" With his temper, his accent deepened. The wildness of his heritage, the untamed quality that still flowed in his veins rose, blotting out what few civilized trappings he had chosen to wear. "A rogue stud for the lady mare?" The hands holding hers tightened.

Caprice froze for one second, then her chin lifted, her own temper matching his. Hers had been no gentle rearing either. She knew how to fight. She knew how to wound. "If I were your equal in strength, you would apologize for that," she hissed, drawing back as far as the hold on her hands would allow. She didn't pit her physical power against his. She never fought unequal battles until she had a shot at winning. "I lie down for no man that way, no matter how much pleasure he promises."

"Then answer the question," he shot back. In her anger, she was his warrior woman, strong enough to accept all that he had been.

"Do I accept you as my stud? No. Do I want to share the night with you? Yes. Will I share this night with you? Over your dead body." She glared at him, too infuriated to even care what her words sounded like or who might step out of the darkness to hear them.

Quin just stared at her, caught by the intensity of emotion pouring out of her. Warrior woman? No. High priestess of the warriors? Yes. The anger drained from his body, stolen by hers. His lips curved at the picture she made as she defied him to do his worst. And she called herself a coward. He was beginning to believe she didn't know the meaning of the word. A chuckle rumbled forth, then another, and suddenly laughter finished the last of his temper. He drew her stiff body to his, ignoring her indignant oath.

"My dead body wouldn't be any good to you at all, little warrior," he murmured, wrapping his arms around her.

Her fists trapped between them, Caprice had little leverage. What she did have she used. She tromped on his instep and pushed. He didn't move, his laughter still embracing her with almost as much fury-stealing warmth as the heat from his body.

"Damn you, let me go, she muttered, wiggling in an attempt to get a better shot at him. Suddenly she stopped in mid-maneuver as she felt his hand slide to the base of her spine. "Don't you dare!"

Pressure, then the delicious shiver of sensation that flowed out from his fingers as they traced the bundle of nerves and tension he found so unerringly. Caprice tried to fight, but she was lost before the next breath. Her body rippled beneath the hands that had shown it such pleasure, arching like a cat waiting to be petted by a favored master. Anger died, killed by passion so swift that it left no traces of anything but wanting in its wake.

"Damn you," Caprice moaned as she lifted her mouth to his.

"Damn me if you must, my woman. But have you I will," he whispered before he took her offering.

Caprice turned from her window, glaring at nothing in particular. Even after four hours, Quin's words were still as hot and full of promise as his touch had been.

"Damn that man!" Caprice flung herself down in the overstuffed chair he had used and promptly found a loose spring that had killer tendencies. Cursing, she hopped up and stomped across the room to the love seat that had seen better days. "Have you I will, will he?" She shifted restlessly on the small couch, trying to ignore the need that wouldn't release her. He had built that fire, fed it enough fuel to destroy her sleep, and then left her at the door with nothing more than a kiss that promised heaven and delivered hell. She wanted him. More accurately, if he had been sitting there, she would have taken him whether he wanted her or not. She had never ached this much, needed this much, wanted so completely that sleep was an impossible dream. She wanted to tell herself it was just sex. But sex didn't brand, claim, possess. It didn't demand more than passion for an hour. It didn't command total attention. It didn't create images that made her writhe in an agony that had nothing to do with pain.

She rose, wrapping her arms around herself. Her hair was a tangled mass down her back, unknowingly wanton, provocative. Her skin was tinged with pink, flushed with the fire that still raged. Her eyes glittered like emerald flares as she paced, stopping at the end of each turn to glare at the number for his hotel that he had given her before he had walked her to her door.

"The next move is yours," she whispered, repeating his last words as she halted in front of the table and picked up the tiny piece of paper. Seven digits. One choice. The question was when. When did she take what she was coming to want more than her next heartbeat? When did she surrender to this man who held darkness in his pale eyes, who spoke of death with poetry and cynicism, who touched her with such shocking desire that no force stood against him?

Tonight. The need was pain-deep and heart-wide. Tomorrow. Cowardice was painted for his eyes and her own. Next week. Loneliness for seven days, one day for every number that would call him to her side. Her hand lifted, her eyes trained on the card she held in the other. The phone was cold, the desire hot.

One number, two, three . . .

One ring, two . . .

"Quinlan." His answer was abrupt, short.

Caprice's fingers tightened on the receiver. Silence. The words wouldn't come.

"Caprice." This time the tone was gentle, soothing, as though Quin had all the time in the world to wait for her surrender.

Caprice swallowed, damning her loss of control. She had made her decision. She would not back down. "Tonight." She paused, then added softly, "I will come to you if you still want me."

"Because of what your body is telling you or your mind?"

Caprice closed her eyes against the question she would rather not have faced. "You want it all, don't you?"

"As you need comfort and security, I need this."

A simple answer from a complicated man. "My body wants you. You made sure that it did," she whispered achingly.

Quin inhaled deeply, feeling the thrust of her truth right to his soul. He had played a card and discovered another held the ace.

"But my mind wants you, too. I don't know why. I don't even want to know why." Tears welled in her eyes. Crying had never been easy for her. It was natural tonight. The tears flowed, clear ribbons of moisture that marked the changes in her. Birth, a process always painful, traumatic.

"I will come and get you."

"You don't have to."

"I want to." He replaced the phone silently without saying goodbye.

Caprice hung up, feeling lighter, more at peace than she could ever remember. She had stepped blindly out, not being certain there was ground beneath her, and now she was flying, cut free from the bonds of earth and responsibilities. She didn't know how long the flight would be, but she would enjoy all it had to offer for as long as it lasted.

Six

The door closed with a soft thud. With the sound, the realization of what she was about to do made itself felt in a flutter of butterfly wings in the pit of her stomach. Caprice turned her back to the muted light of the sitting room. "I'm nervous," she murmured. "I didn't expect to be."

Quin came to her, not touching her yet. He knew what he was asking of her. He could have use passion to ease the moment, but he respected her too much for that kind of trick. "Do you want to change your mind?"

She searched his eyes, seeing the desire that he made no attempt to hide. He would let her leave, take her back to her apartment if she asked. Her decision as he had insisted it be. "No." She touched the tip of her tongue to her dry lips. His gaze followed the movement as he closed the last inches that separated them. "I want you."

His lips curved into a smile that held promise of pleasure to come and knowledge of what it had cost her to offer herself. "As much as I want you, I wonder?" He cupped her face in his warm palms, his fingers tracing her mouth as though he would tactilely paint the full curves. He bent his head, his kiss trailing the lines drawn by his touch. "Close your eyes."

"Why?" she whispered even as she obeyed.

"For darkness. For secrets that you will learn. Secrets I will teach." He slid his hands through her hair, massaging her scalp, finding the nerves that would release the tension coiled so tightly in her.

Caprice sighed deeply, feeling herself unravel from the inside out. His warmth was all around her, his scent exotic, teasing her. Her lashes shut, she was locked in a world she had never known, a world he was creating with each new caress. His hands eased down the back of her neck, probing deeply, leaving a strange lassitude in their wake. She swayed. His arms held her steady, suspended between earth and sky. And still he stroked her, lower, her shoulders now, her arms, which she hadn't realized she had wrapped around his waist.

"Quin." His name was a plea that she made gladly.

His kiss sealed her lips. "Silence," he whispered.

He lifted her so slowly into his arms that she felt as though she floated close to his heart by thought alone. Her head dropped to his shoulder, too heavy now for her to hold erect. She nuzzled his throat, her tongue flicking out to taste him, to savor the scent and the man. His arms contracted, leaving the feeling of being free a memory. She was chained to him and that, too, was right. The darkness deepened. Something solid beneath her back. The bed?

Quin gazed down at her as she lay before him. There was just enough light from the slightly ajar bathroom door that permitted only the faintest ray of illumination to reach the bed. For a moment, he memorized the picture she made, her limbs in an elegant sprawl, her skin flushed with pleasure and building need, her eyes shut, her breath slipping from one inhalation to the next in a relaxed flow. No fear touched her now. She was alive and his.

He reached down without taking his eyes from her face. Her joy would be mirrored there. His pleasure would be doubled with her delight. Wrapping his fingers around her ankles, he slipped her shoes, one at a time, from her feet.

Caprice moaned softly in the stillness as he touched her, his hands once again probing deep into her flesh. She lost the concept of time as her clothes slipped away from her, as he stroked each inch of her skin until she was positive her body had dissolved into a soft mass of warmth. Then his touch changed, caressing, shaping, defining her. She was a creation, his creation, molded and formed by his fingers into a woman she had never known. Alive, vibrating with awareness of herself and every nuance of the world he had built around her. As he discovered her, she learned much from him. Desire was no urgent scream for fulfillment. Rather, it was an achingly exquisite slide into sensation that held more life and energy than anything she had ever known. Her body was no vulnerable shell only breathing for survival. It was a beautiful entity with gossamer wings to explore the heavens, to feel everything, to have the keys to all riddles.

"Quin." His name came in a voice she didn't recognize.

But Quin heard. His breath warmed her lips. "Not yet."

"Please." She tried to open her eyes and discovered she could not. "Join with me."

Quin cupped her breasts, the first truly sexual touch he had given her. His thumbs rasped lightly across her nipples. Her body rippled in response, shivers flowing over her, telling him how very ready for his possession she was. Releasing her with one hand, he unbuttoned his shirt. The hair on his chest was strangely dark and thick. But she didn't see. He leaned forward, nestling breasts into his chest as he took her lips. Her sigh of pleasure was deep, sweet, and all he had imagined.

Caprice lifted her arms, binding him close. "Clothes. Make them go away."

He laughed softly. Even in her need, she commanded. "Some."

"All." She arched suddenly as his hand slid down her belly into the soft blond curls that guarded her modesty. She gasped as his fingers found the center of her, stroking the tiny bud of femininity. Then he probed deeper, filling her and the world of darkness. With no warning, the darkness was split, ripped apart by flames. She cried out, branding the silence with one word.

"Quin!"

She soared, past the heavens into the universe and still the flames followed. She flew past the sun, scorched with the heat and the fire. Her arms tightened, holding on to Quin, her only security in a world being reborn. Her nails raked his shirt, tearing at the cloth. Then the darkness returned in a rush that caught her unprepared for its complete power. Oblivion. The fire died.

Quin bent his head to touch her lips as she lay curled in his arms, caught in the boneless, thoughtless limbo following ecstasy. She was vulnerable now. He could do anything with her and she would obey him blindly. To give her more than she had ever known he had brought her to this. But he would not take. Not ever. Gently, tenderly he laid her back, pulling the sheet over her to guard against the coolness of the room. Her senses were satiated, for a moment too lazy to do their job of maintaining her body's needs. She would feel heat and cold too easily. Pain and pleasure, too.

"You're safe," he murmured, bending close to her, his breath warming her lips.

"Safe." Her mouth formed the words but no sound emerged. The dream that never came true. Even in the mindless state of total possession, she remembered that.

Quin leaned back and took off his shoes and slacks without moving from her side. Then, shirt still on, he slipped under the sheet and eased her up onto his chest. He brushed back the hair from her face and lifted her chin for his kiss. He probed delicately at her lips until they opened for him. As he deepened the kiss, he joined with her in one smooth stroke. Moist heat surrounded him, pulling him in as though he had come home from a long journey.

Caprice forced her eyes open. "Finally," she breathed faintly. "I feel full."

"Do you, my warrior maid?" He lifted his hips, increasing the mating to his full length.

Caprice exhaled in pleasure, curling around him, her hands holding him as though he would disappear. "So good."

"Soon it will be better."

"Can't."

He smiled, his eyes glittering with a need that was almost savage. Desire had razor claws to scar. He accepted each slash of denied relief as he stroked her slowly, tending with care the fire he had brought to her. He watched her face, listened to the language of her body, and gave all they asked and more. He felt each snap of the chain links as, one by one, he and his woman broke the last of human restraint. His movements quickened and Caprice kept pace. He arched toward her as she gave herself completely.

"Mine," he groaned hoarsely as he gave himself to her in one wild thrust that, for endless moments, did the impossible. They were one, one body, one thought, one sensation, one soul. Belonging.

Caprice lay spent on his chest, her face pressed against his heart, his arms wrapped around her. Sleep beckoned like a gentle breeze to refresh and revive. She resisted for one moment. She raised her head, her senses still caught in the sensual web he had spun for her. If she had not needed to speak so desperately, she would not have been able to force the effort from her body. Her fingers shook as she touched his lips but she didn't notice.

"You are magic," she murmured faintly. "A strange magic that no man can have and still be of this world." She tried to read his expression but she was just so weary. Exhausted by her exertion, she let her lashes close. "Am I magic, too?" she asked just before sleep possessed her as surely as Quin had done.

Quin's arms tightened around her. "Many things I have been called, woman of mine," he replied, his accent more evident than he would have allowed with anyone else. "But never magic. I am only a man with a very great need that only you can fill." He eased her against his side and pulled the covers over them. Sleep would come this night as a friend, and it was because of her.

Caprice awakened by degrees. First, she felt the weight of the arms that held her, then the heat of his body, and finally the lightness of her own. She smiled softly as she opened her eyes to a new day. The room was cool, dim, a haven. She turned her head to look at Quin as he lay beside her. She studied his face, taking advantage of the rare opportunity to look at him with his guard

down. Even in repose his strength was evident. The dark shadow
of his beard surprised her a little considering the lightness of his
hair and eyes. Her gaze traveled lower, suddenly focusing on the
shirt collar framing his throat. She frowned, lifting a hand to touch
it as though she couldn't believe it existed. His fingers curled
around hers.

"It doesn't matter," he murmured.

Caprice looked up, her curiosity clear. "But why?"

"My back is scarred."

She glanced at the hand holding hers. "Like these?" She stroked
them lightly, gently.

"Worse," he said flatly.

Caprice studied the torn flesh, listening beyond the words that
said he accepted his flawed body. Was he afraid she would turn
away from him? As others had done? Could he be hurt that deeply?
The poet could. But the cynic and the realist? Logic held no answer. And he certainly would give her none. The decision was
hers. Instinct whispered softly. She bent her head slowly, her hair
falling delicately around her face, shielding her and what she intended from his sight. Her lips brushed the deepest scar. His hand
tightened in shock. Rejection? She traced the line to the next
wound. Still, he did not draw away even though she could feel the
tension invading his body. She soothed the next mark, then the
next, her lips easing slowly, inevitably to his shirt cuff. She unbuttoned it without pausing in her task, pushing it up until it would
go no farther. When she kissed the last inch of damaged skin, she
raised her head.

Quin stared at her, the silver rain of hair framing her face and
flowing over his chest. No woman had ever touched him in such
a way. He felt heat that had nothing to do with passion burn away
some of the pain of the wounds that had healed but never disap-
peared from flesh or memory.

Caprice felt the tension leave his body in one deep sigh. She
had won this war, not with words but with gentleness. "Last night
you took me in a way I have never known. I was yours. You could
have asked anything of me and I would have given it to you. I
trusted you as I have trusted no one else."

He read the need in her eyes, the hope as well. "You want me
to take it off."

She nodded. "I won't promise you I won't react. I will promise you that it won't be because of the disfigurement. It will be what I will see that you've suffered."

He wanted to believe her. This dragon had been more silent than most, and until he had looked into her clear eyes, he hadn't even realized how strong it was, the fire it could breathe to sear mind and heart. "You don't know how bad it is."

She smiled, her gaze tender. "You never exaggerate. If it is this bad to you, it's bad." She lifted herself to reach his mouth. Her kiss was a plea and a command. She leaned back to look at him. Her gaze was steady, committed. "Please."

"You said that last night."

"And I'll probably say it again." She pulled away from him, giving him room to sit up. When he did and reached for the edges of the, shirt, she stopped him with a touch. "Close your eyes.

He searched her face. "Why?"

"Because I ask it of you."

"So you can hide?"

She shook her head, her hands replacing his on the shirt. "No. So you can. We all need to, sometimes. Darkness is good if you have someone to share it with. You shared mine last night. Let me share yours."

He held her gaze, wondering at the depths he had missed in his need to make her his. How did she know how much he was already hating what he would find in her expression when she saw the ugly web of destruction that marred his flesh? If she cared for him, she would get used to the sight. But he would also carry the memory of this moment. Trust. It had been so long, perhaps forever, since he had trusted anyone this much. Slowly, his lashes drifted shut.

Caprice's sigh of relief was clearly audible in the dark silence. "Thank you."

Her kiss feathered across his lips even as he felt the shirt slide down his arms. The mattress dipped as she rose beside him.

Caprice stared in horror at the long, cruel furrows in his skin. Pain wouldn't have begun to describe what he had survived. Agony, enough to scream, would have been closer. She didn't feel the first drops of her tears as she leaned forward and rested her cheek against the worst of the damage.

Quin stiffened at her touch. An instant later, every bit of tension

drained from the body that had survived the sadistic hand of man.
Tears. He could feel them dripping down his back as his blood once
had. Healing. His eyes opened. He thought of his dragons and the
woman he had been promised would slay them. Tears. One of her
weapons. He turned, pulling her against his chest as she burrowed
close, her arms wrapping around him as though she would physically
shield him from hurt. He stroked her hair as she cried out his pain
against his heart. For every tear, he murmured words in a language
that no longer existed. Finally, when she was spent, he tilted her
head back to look into her red-rimmed eyes. Her beauty was magnified by her gift. He touched the last tear starring her lashes.

"Come to me. Forget the year you promised," he pleaded
hoarsely. He would have said those words, asked that of no other
on the face of the earth or heaven itself but Caprice.

His need was strong but no stronger than her own. When he
held her, she felt whole. When he touched her, the magic breathed
life and loving. When he smiled at her, she believed in dreams.
But she had made a promise to a woman and man who had come
to her when she had had nothing, no present, no future, no hope,
only an endless succession of days to survive.

"I can't. My mother was right. I have to find what is important.
She started it, but you have shown me how much I have missed."

Even as he honored her strength, he denied it with a plea and
a protest. "I can show you more." He stroked her breasts lightly,
teasing the nipples to remind her of what they had found in each
other's arms.

Caprice covered his hand, stilling his touch, reinforcing his
claim to her. "And I will let you. Here, if you will or can stay."

Every emotion Quin possessed demanded he wring a agreement
out of her. His own honor and sense of justice commanded he
give her the time she had promised her mother. He had been given
and chosen a woman with a power to match his own. To wish her
less was to devalue what each of them was. "I hate where you're
living. At least let me rent us an apartment."

She shook her head, sensing his capitulation. "I told you the
terms. That wouldn't be keeping to them." His curse might have
been in a language she didn't understand, but it sounded amazingly
graphic. She smiled, covering his lips with her fingers. "Would
you break your word if you had given it?"

"No, damn you, I wouldn't. But don't expect me to like what you're asking," he replied bluntly.

She laughed, hugging him. She hadn't known he could react so irritably. His control was paper thin this morning. Because of her and what they had shared? She hoped so. She could feel the changes occurring within her. She didn't want to believe she was the only one being affected by their sharing. "Are we going to do more of what we did last night?" she demanded, tipping back her head to challenge him.

"Soothing the savage beast?" His light brows lifted mockingly.

"Definitely. As well as filling a emptiness that is aching for just one man," she whispered daringly. "And while we're at it, you can teach me a few of those wickedly delicious tricks of yours."

His eyes gleamed as his hands moved, touching her in new places. "Those kinds of tricks."

Caprice shifted as sensations raced through her, awakening the need once more. "You know it," she replied, trying to duplicate the caress he had just given her.

Whether it was blind luck or intent, she didn't know. But his sudden stillness, followed by a deep groan that held as much surprise as pleasure, told her that she had scored at least one hit dead center on target. Probing delicately, she closed her eyes, speaking to him through her fingers. For every touch of his, she followed until suddenly the world shifted and he took her to the mattress in a controlled rush that bore no resemblance to the orchestrated passion of the night.

They came together in one deep thrust. Her arms wrapped around him, caging him as she tied herself to him for the flight to come. They sliced through time and space, hurtling toward completion at a rate that neither could control or stop. Then suddenly, they were there. Caught in a fire that consumed and birthed as one. When it was over, silence and the future neither had anticipated waited to receive them.

Seven

"Why don't you let me help you get another job?" Quin demanded irritably, watching Caprice study the newspaper carefully. They had breakfasted together for the last four days, and every morning had been a replay of the same. She circled ads and dressed for interviews, and he killed time until she returned still minus a job.

Caprice looked up, shaking her head. "We've had this discussion before. I agreed to the rules. I'll play by them. Silke made it."

"Killian helped her," Quin muttered, goaded into betraying the truth.

Caprice's eyes narrowed. She put down the paper very carefully. "What do you mean he helped her? I can't believe that. Silke wouldn't have cheated."

"She didn't cheat. She didn't know."

Caprice thought that over, looking for answers in his eyes. But this morning, unlike others, secrets lived where passion and openness had once reigned. "Just what did Killian do? And why was he doing anything? As far as I know, he had never met Silke before."

Quin rose, coffee cup in hand, to go to the tiny stove for a refill. Killian had not told him everything about his association with the St. James family prior to his marriage to Silke—only those things he had needed to know to help Killian save Silke's life. What blanks had been left, Quin had filled in for himself. His conclusion was there was a damn good chance Kill's company had been hired either to watch over the St. James daughters or to actively help them create new lives in the supposed real world.

"Well?" Caprice demanded, when he didn't reply.

Quin turned around, cup in hand, and leaned against the counter. "He didn't tell me he had met her before," he answered honestly. "I do know that he spoke to his friend, Spike Douglas, the owner of Douglas Plastics, about her. I do know that she got a job for which she had no experience. Maybe I added wrong."

Caprice frowned, searching for the off-color thread in the tapestry of his words. He was leaving something out. "And?"

He shrugged. "And nothing. You commented on the unlikeliness of Killian seeking outside work."

"You think he was in Atlanta because of Silke?"

"Yes."

"But why?"

He shrugged again.

Caprice turned the idea over in her mind. Her father often remarked on her agile thought processes, and right now they were shouting some very disturbing messages. "It doesn't make sense."

"The man following you every day does."

She focused on his face, seeing the grim curve of his lips, the intent look that spelled trouble. "How do you know?"

"I followed him following you."

"And?"

"He carries a gun and a permit for it. Along with a driver's license for the state of Pennsylvania."

Caprice considered his revelations. Oddly, discovering that Quin had followed her didn't bother her as much as thinking her family had felt she needed a watchdog or guard or whatever Killian's tail was. "Are you saying he works for Killian?"

"It's a good bet." Quin returned to his chair, slightly surprised that Caprice was not objecting to his shadowing of her. "Is it likely that your family would have sent you and your sisters out on your own without, at least, trying to protect you?"

"But the whole point was to make it so that we all had to rely on our own resources," she protested. Even as she said the words she was beginning to believe what they were both thinking was the truth of the situation.

"Silke did. You are. I would imagine Leora and Noelle are as well."

"You just said Silke didn't."

"No. I said she had help. Successful businessmen, even in the name of friendship, don't keep on idiots no matter how small the capacity. And especially when a company is trying to establish itself in a new territory. Silke did her job or she wouldn't have had it." He waited a moment, then added bluntly, "So I'm asking you to let me pull a few strings to get you past the screening process. You know damn well that degree you've supposedly never used and your equally fictitious lack of any kind of work experience are killing your chances of anything but the kind of job you had at Billy's."

"No."

He swore once.

"If you're going to lose your temper, at least do it in a language I understand," she shot back. "I'm no hothouse plant that has to be sheltered, regardless of what my family thinks. And while we're on the subject, why did you follow me in the first place?"

"No. You're a stubborn, willful, temperamental female who has more honor than sense," he retaliated irritably. He glared at her. "As for following you, it wasn't because I didn't believe you could take care of yourself, if that's what you're thinking. You forgot the newspaper the other day, remember? I caught you just before you turned into the street. I saw a car I've seen downstairs twice before. I've spent too many years watching my back not to recognize something out of sync."

Tension drained out of her with his explanation. Caprice grinned, his comment not close to touching her anger. "Nice way to talk about your lover."

"I don't feel nice." Contempt layered the last word. "And I damn well won't act nice if you end up at another Billy's. And that's final." He rose from his chair in one smooth lift, reached across the table, plucked her up, and hauled her against him before she had time to do more than blink in surprise.

"What are you doing?" she demanded, tipping back her head to glare at him. Any amusement was gone the moment she looked into his eyes. He was serious, too serious for play.

"I'm warning you. I won't watch you get hurt. I promised you honesty, but I didn't promise to stand by and let you run wild enough for that. I will protect you and I will help you. You gave me those rights whether you knew it or not when you gave me your body." He cupped her breast, stroking the tip in a way that he knew would bring alive the fire that still lay smoldering within her. His own body reacted as swiftly, taught by her to need as she needed.

Caprice trembled against him, helpless to dam the flow of passion quickening deep in her belly. Even as she realized her own vulnerability she felt her strength. He was no less affected by the caress than she, no less a prisoner of the desire that burned white-hot between them. "I have never had a protector before," she said huskily as she reached up to touch his cheek. His eyes glittered like polished silver. "I've never felt I could give in to that kind of dependency."

"I'm not trying to steal your strength, only augment it," he replied roughly, willing her to understand.

Caprice studied his face, the unrelenting purpose that tightened the planes and angles that made up his features. He was trying to meet her halfway, but he was also telling her he had compromised as far as he would. If she didn't accept his offer, she risked tearing apart the fragile trust that was building between them. That, more than the exquisite passion he could call at will, decided her. "All right. Pull your strings. But only as far as getting my foot in the door." She traced his lips and the curve of satisfaction that softened them. "But if I find out you've done any more than that, I'll make you wish you had never put your fingers in my particular pie."

Quin kissed the tips of her fingers, smiling at her fierce expression. "I believe you," he murmured, laughing softly. Now that he had her agreement, he could afford humor.

"But I'm not giving up this apartment," Caprice added in case he got the wrong idea about her capitulation.

"I figured that out on my own." Using one arm, he lifted her off her feet and over his shoulder.

Disoriented, Caprice was slow to react. She grabbed his belt to steady herself, blew her hair out of her eyes, and swore roundly. "What are you doing?"

"Taking you to bed."

"What?" She thumped him on the back. "Put me down. I am not . . ." The last of her words were lost as he dumped her on her back on the mattress. The force of the drop stole her breath for the crucial seconds it took for him to come down beside her.

"Don't fight me. I need to hold you," he said, as he draped a thigh over hers and cupped her chin in his palm. He stared into her irritated, disbelieving eyes and whispered, "I'm not accustomed to giving in. And I am finding I am very possessive where you are concerned."

She felt the need in him that he was clearly trying to control for her sake. She wondered at its strength even as she accepted the magnitude of it. "You can't chain me to the bed."

"If I thought it would work, I would," he stated bluntly. He stroked her length, making no move to divest her of her clothes.

Caprice trembled with the sweep of his hand. "You don't need this to bring me to heel. I want to stay with you, work with you." She shook her head against the pillow, loosening the last mooring of pins so that the remaining tendrils escaped with the movement. "I have never told any man that."

Quin searched her clear eyes, reading the truth. He sighed deeply, relieved. "I had hoped."

She smiled faintly. "I'm glad you care." Simple words, complex emotion. She touched the first button of his shirt. "I really do need to hit the interview trail. But if you are determined to spend the day in bed . . ."

It was his turn to shake his head. "Let me make a few calls first." He waited.

"It will cost you."

"Name it."

"Lunch. Someplace expensive. I'm dying for a steak. Maybe lobster."

He grinned, his eyes gleaming with a gypsy's boldness. "With luck, we'll make it a celebration meal."

"I have to see some results first." She lifted her head to kiss him quickly, then slid out from under his leg and scrambled off the bed.

Quin watched her smooth her clothes, admiring her body as much as her mind. She intrigued him with all the twists and turns that made up her personality. She kept him constantly on his toes as he tried to out-think and out-gun her.

"What I want to know is how you know anyone here when you told me you've never been in the city before," Caprice said absently as she walked to the tarnished mirror on the wall to check her hair. As usual it was coming down around her ears.

Quin stiffened, then relaxed when he realized Caprice had no idea what door she had just opened—a door to a room filled with more lies than truth. "There are a number of large corporations here. Those and some of the people who run them I do know." He got to his feet, his eyes on the unconsciously sensual movements she made as she repaired her hair and makeup. Women held few mysteries for him, so few in fact that, beyond the satisfaction of his body's needs and theirs, he had no real interest in what else they did. Until Caprice. Everything she did or thought held value. He wanted to watch her when she was doing nothing more than sleeping. He wanted to hear her ideas even if they were simple ones about mundane things.

Caprice smiled at him in the cloudy mirror before turning to face him. "Are you trying to tell me you have clout?"

He shrugged. "Of a kind. In your case, the necessary kind."

"That sounds like double-talk." She frowned a little, suddenly realizing that, although they had discussed her life at length and in depth, the same could not be said for Quin. She hadn't questioned him very deeply after he had told her about his family, in spite of the fact that she had thought about it. But other things had gotten in the way in each case. Her questions had lived only in her mind. "How can a man who solves puzzles have that kind of power?"

"You know I did other things before that."

She tried not to think of the few hints he had given her to that other life. "You made your power base then?"

He had told lies for any number of reasons over the years, told them without a blink to people who had some claim on him. But he couldn't look at Caprice and do the same. This was a weakness when he thought he no longer had them. He turned and headed for the door. "You could say that."

Caprice's frown deepened as she followed. "What is it you don't want to tell me?" she asked as he reached for the phone on the small table in the living room. He was closing her out, and it hurt in ways that surprised her.

Quin glanced briefly over his shoulder, knowing he was putting off this moment of partial truth for as long as he could. He had been able to evade most of her probing, but he had always known he was living on borrowed and stolen time. One day she would have to know the full truth. Turning from her and the questions in her eyes, he pulled his personal address book from his inside pocket. The pages were covered in his own brand of code, difficult and time-consuming for any unfriendly eyes to unscramble. Another old habit that still had a use in this life.

"You haven't told me everything about your past," he pointed out as he found the number he sought.

"All the things that matter," she replied, startled at the comment. She sat down, watching him as he spoke to the person he had called. In a few words, with a slight change in his speech pattern, he suddenly transformed himself into a stranger. He was brisk, abrupt almost, as he made her credentials clear and his own support evident. Then he listened, rejecting whatever was being said. Silence, the kind that he did best. Then the party on the other end of the connection surrendered. He hung up with only a word of thanks and then jotted down whatever information had been given. He swung around, not speaking for a moment, the paper that represented her immediate future in his hand.

Caprice didn't like the silence. Something about it made her think of danger, things best left undiscovered. "You made it sound as if you had known me forever," she said finally, needing a link with ordinary things.

Quin's expression didn't change as he watched her. "You would rather I had said we had a relationship?" He returned his address book to its place without taking his eyes from hers. He could read curiosity in the emerald seas, but no fear, at least not yet. His body tightened at the realization that was being forced on it. In the not too distant tomorrow, he just might have to face that closing down, that regret for what they had shared. Night after day. Cold after warmth. A cage after freedom. Each gained its strength by the very fact it existed to define the other. If he could not keep her, his world would be a cold, dark cage.

"You know I wouldn't have. Not that I am ashamed of us, but they would make something out of it."

He inclined his head, watching, waiting.

Now, she recognized the silence for what it was. A showdown of a sort. She had a choice to pursue her curiosity or back off. She wondered which would do less damage. "I think I need to know all the answers to all the questions I haven't asked," she murmured finally.

Quin felt the instincts that had saved his life on more than one occasion rise to the surface. He braced himself, expecting nothing and everything. "I will be the same man who gave you pleasure," he pointed out, sparing neither of them.

Caprice held his look, suddenly aware that something was changing and it wasn't just the phone call that had created the metamorphosis. Quin was no longer the man who had followed her to Houston. This man was more dangerous, more capable of things that were spoken of only in whispers, if at all. Fear trickled through her, fear of what these next few moments would bring rather than fear of the man himself. She glanced to the scars on his hands, the image of those on his back even more vivid.

"You're beginning to understand." He jammed his hands in his pockets, a reflex that was almost as much a part of him as the silver eyes that had followed him through many lives.

For one instant, Caprice almost faltered. He had given her a taste of heaven. Could she really dare the hell that had spawned the cruelty that still marked his body? "Tell me," she whispered at last, knowing that, in reality, there was no other choice. They had come too far for anything less.

"I won't let you go," he said harshly. "I have found you. I won't let you walk away."

She shivered at the intensity of his voice and the blaze of purpose in his eyes. She didn't doubt he would move mountains and seas to keep her. His was a rage to possess that should have frightened her. Instead, all she could see was his emptiness and her own.

"I'll take the chance."

"Certainty." She had to know he would not release her. She had to see that his choice was more than words born in passion.

"I understand."

He studied her in grim silence, reading the belief she still had in herself to hold him at bay if that was what she decided. It was a wish and belief born in ignorance of the man he was. In this, there was no way to protect her.

"Tonight."

She shook her head. "Now." The rejection in his eyes was diamond hard. "Please."

He closed his eyes. That one word. Their word. She had told him she would use it again, but he had never thought to find it here. "All right." He opened his lashes, looking at her for one moment, memorizing what was and might never be again, not in the same way, with the same trust and belief in herself, her judgment, him.

He glanced past her to the window, staring at the horizon. "Short and to the point. I was a mercenary of a kind. A hired gun, hired mind, and hired skill. I'm good at what I do. Silent. Accurate and expensive. Most of the time I was on the so-called good guys' side, but that was, especially in the beginning, a matter of luck rather than intent."

Caprice studied his stiff back, the harsh words self-damning. She ached for him, the pain she could sense leashed in every syllable. She took a step toward him. Her experiences gave her what other women did not have—compassion that saw beyond society's ideas of right and wrong and understanding of the need to survive despite the odds. She touched his back.

"I'm still here," she murmured quietly. Her lashes flickered as he flinched before turning to face her. His eyes searched her expression as though he believed she lied. "You won't drive me away with your past. But you will help me to see you."

"I'm not trying to drive you away," he denied abruptly. He caught her shoulders and brought her to him. "That's the last thing I want."

Caprice tipped back her head. "Then stop condemning yourself and tell me the whole thing instead of making announcements while you dare me to accept them. Tell me how you went from being recruited by a military man to being a mercenary."

He sighed deeply, holding her close, absorbing her presence in ways he didn't want to explain. "It's a long story."

"So we'll miss lunch." She stirred in his arms, raising her head from his shoulder. "But let's not do it standing up." She pulled away, taking his hand, scars and all, and urging him toward the lumpy love seat.

Quin stared at the link between them, knowing there was no other woman who would have handled his history in just this way. The prophecy had been right, although over the years he had almost convinced himself that it had been an old man's wanderings. Obeying the pull on his arm, he sat down beside her, waiting for her to let go. But she didn't. Her fingers entwined with his, she waited, her eyes clear, bright, and fearless.

"I thought I understood you," he murmured.

She smiled. "I know. I thought I understood myself." She shook her head, laughing gently at both of them. "We're learning things together." Her humor died. "Now, tell me. All of it. Not just the ugly parts that paint you dark. But the full range of it."

"I was recruited. Four years of special training. I liked the discipline but not as much as I hated the loss of freedom. The politics of the situation didn't matter to me, but the way this particular army conducted its business did. My sister wasn't the only casualty. The moment my commitment was at an end, I signed out. It wasn't easy. The man who had brought me in had other plans and tried to fix it so that I had to stay. I'd made some friends of a sort. They helped me escape the trap he laid."

Caprice squeezed his lingers, offering silent comfort. She wanted to fill in a few blanks with questions, but the swirls of anger, frustration, and disillusionment in his eyes held her mute.

"My 'friends' were hired guns. I suspected it before I accepted their help, but the alternative was becoming a military rapist and killer of innocents. So I took a chance and incurred a debt that had to be paid. I worked with them, taking the chances they took, living the life they lived. At first, the association worked. The group was more idealistic than most, ex-military with an eye to helping the underdog. Then the leader was killed. And a new man, one who didn't care about human life and freedom, took over. He sold us to the highest bidder without discussing it with the group first. The money was better than we had ever made. The ideals went down without a whimper." He touched her face with his free hand. "Only two of the four men who had helped me escape still lived. I had a feeling that the setup wasn't right. I went on that first raid. They died. I came back, just long enough to collect my gear. After that I worked alone. I made my choices based on the employer's need and money. Politics still meant nothing to me. But freedom did. No one deserved to be chained by a government made of men no better and usually far worse than they."

His lips twisted into a grim curve. "In spite of the fact I often worked for the underdog, the pay was better than good. By the time I was thirty, I was a millionaire five times over. I was also tired. I'd had a bellyful of lies, tricks, and looking over my shoulder. So I walked away. I took my money and bought an island and a new life. This time, freedom was really mine to command. No debts to pay that required my walking into a cage not of my choosing. No rules to follow but those that I made. No world to intrude unless I wished it."

"So you cut yourself off from human need as I did."

"It's not the same. Damn it, I could have been something better. Hell, I've spent the last seven years of my life realizing that. Do you think I like knowing it?"

She felt the rage building in him, accepting it as she accepted him. She caught his face, her hands on each side, her eyes holding his. "I think you have made yourself guilty for what you don't believe, don't feel, don't count as valuable. Everyone has a right to those things. Is believing in one government all that perfect? By your own admission, you picked your sides based on what you perceived as right. As far as I'm concerned, that's more honorable than fighting a war you don't believe in for the sake of citizenship in a country."

Quin watched her eyes, searching for the faintest flicker of un-truth. She didn't condemn as he had expected. "I am not who I said I am," he admitted finally, realizing that this time the partial truth had to be made whole. She had given him more than he thought he deserved. It was only right that he return the gift to the giver.

Caprice stroked his hair at his left temple. His pulse beat strongly beneath her fingers. "A woman, even one who has made her life the corporate fast lane, can recognize a dye job, even if it is a good one like this. I'll admit I didn't figure it out immediately. What color was it?"

"Black."

"You have enemies still, don't you?" She thought of the scars, of the hatred that would have driven the hand that had made them. Fear came swiftly, stark, unstoppable. Her lashes lowered as she fought the feeling. He would not see that her fear was for him, only that it existed. She hadn't seen him as a man who could be hurt. She had been wrong. The poet, the cynic, and the realist were all vulnerable, each in different ways. He had laid his soul at her feet, a gift that had no equal. She would draw her last breath before she put one more invisible scar on its wounded surface.

"Too many." Quin absorbed her warmth. He had taken risks all of his life. Death held little meaning for him any longer. But life, this life, this moment, with Caprice made him want again, want something more than his freedom, something more even than the passion and the woman who had brought it to him. He wanted completion, a closing of the circle of energy that began with time itself. Caprice could offer him that. She held the seed of his own future within her body, his heart within her soul, and his desire within her mind. The fusion of two into one had begun. If she walked away now, he would be half a man, doomed by his own hand to wander the corridors of space and hours, truly alone and forever chained to what could have been.

Caprice opened her eyes, looking into the pale depths of his. A man with his skill would know how to hide. She looked beyond the obvious for the camouflage that had to exist. "A different name?"

"That, too, more than one."

"Are you at risk when you leave your island?"

"A little but not that much. I would not have come to you if I had believed I brought you danger as well as passion." He bent, taking her lips with a kiss that held his promise. "I've been out of the business a long time in the scheme of things, and a great many of those who would know me are probably dead by now." For one second he remembered the enemy far greater than the others who still lived and hunted. But it had been years since Gustaf had been close to finding him. He hadn't relaxed his guard, but he had begun to believe this life was strong enough to survive.

Caprice released her tension with a sigh. If he said it was so, she had to believe him.

Quin covered her hands with his, the light unkind to the scars on his skin. He had to be certain, to have the words that would make the past truly that—the past. "You can live with knowing what I have been?"

Caprice lifted her head, pressing her lips to the back of his right hand. She looked up, daring him to reject her or her judgment. "You aren't perfect. But I never asked you to be." She paused, asking the one question that had to be answered. "Will you be doing it again?"

He shook his head. "Never."

Her smile broke, tension that had wound itself too tight at the first revelation slowly releasing its grip. "Then I can live with it."

Quin shuddered as he sighed deeply. Another dragon slain and this one of the greatest. "I won't forget this," he murmured as he brought her face close for his kiss. For a moment, he savored the simple taste of her lips to his. The fire was a gentle ember that owed its life to her belief and his acceptance. Fragile, the flame need tending. And he was ready to give that care. The prophecy was more than promised, more than hoped. He had reached for the future and found keys to the past. Caprice.

Eight

Quin stared at the exit through which Caprice had to pass to reach the parking lot. He didn't glance at his watch. His sense of time was excellent, so he knew it was well after five, Caprice's quitting time. Not that she seemed to pay any attention to that. Since she had landed the job here at Martinville's, she had changed. Caprice had been supplanted by C. R. Her voice was brisk now, as it had been those first few days in Atlanta. Her walk was sharp—long strides that commanded the eyes. Her clothes and hairstyle were equally geared for the rising young executive. He didn't like the change but hadn't told her that so far. Instead, he had played a waiting game, waiting for her to see what she transformed herself into to worship at her particular god's feet, waiting for her to see the time her drive for success stole from her life, and waiting for her to see what that kind of life was doing to her personality. Three long weeks and he was still waiting. But no longer. His hands clenched in a need for action, his eyes narrowed with purpose.

His decision wasn't based on jealousy, although, much to his surprise, that had been one of his first responses and the main reason he had bided his time. He had calmed the jealousy, not controlled it, by remembering her past and the needs that it had created in her to secure her present. He had been able to view her metamorphosis with more realistic eyes, more understanding. But nothing had changed the facts. Like himself, C. R. was a creature of her experiences, her choices molded by a strangle hold that she was now strong enough to counter.

Suddenly she was there, walking toward him, briefcase in hand, that tilt to her head silently proclaiming she was ready to take on the world. He watched her stride, reading the weariness that dogged her steps, the exhaustion that no one but he or someone who cared about her would have seen. He got out of the car, going around to her side to open the door.

Caprice smiled at him as she dropped her case on the back cushion before sliding into the passenger seat. "Have you been waiting long?" Caprice asked tiredly as she leaned back. She sighed deeply, feeling the tension of the day ease a little. Establishing herself in a new arena was costing her more than she had expected. But she was making progress. She frowned a little, thinking of the innuendos that had come her way in the last few weeks—tacky comments about her figure, hair, and height. She had become inured to those kind of things in Philly, mainly because her exposure had been limited by her father's name and reputation. Only fools with a death wish messed with an aging eagle's child, she thought with a sudden pang of homesickness.

Quin watched the changes of expression, catching glimpses of Caprice behind the facade of C. R. When she frowned, he reached out and plucked free the pins anchoring her hair in a neat twist.

"What are you doing?" she protested, not reacting fast enough to escape his maneuver.

"Bringing Caprice back. I miss her," he murmured as the silken strands flowed like gentle silver rain down her shoulders and back. He slid his fingers through the long length to her scalp, feeling the tension in her. "The things you do to your hair make me angry."

Caprice wrapped her hand around his wrist as she leaned her head into his magic fingers. "You sound like Silke," she whispered. Her lashes drifted shut as he smoothed and stroked her skin, stealing the anxieties of the day with every touch. "That feels good."

"Why do you do this to yourself?" he demanded roughly, although his voice was soft enough not to destroy the tension-relieving atmosphere he was deliberating creating for her.

"It goes with the territory. Except for my height, I look like the proverbial dumb blonde. And no matter how much I would like to deny it, this world is still operating on the male standard."

"So you garb yourself in your armor, tie up this glorious hair, and do battle every day for money you don't need, will never need."

She opened her eyes, smiling faintly at the anger smoldering in his eyes. "You named it well. Like your puzzles, it's what I do."

He shook his head, his hand stilling. "No. It's what you become." With his free hand he touched the tightly buttoned up blouse, the man-cut jacket, and utilitarian watch. "This is C. R., not Caprice. I don't like it." He stroked her lips before she could protest. "And you shouldn't either. It isn't you, at least not now. It may never have been."

Caprice stared at him, realizing that this was no simple, easily shrugged-off comment. He meant every word. She could have fought him if he had demanded out of his need alone that she change. But he didn't. He was holding up a mirror for her to see herself as he could see her. She thought of the two nights before she and her sisters had left Philadelphia. She had been imbibing Silke's vodka too freely, a first. She had felt reckless that night, determined to alter the course of her life. Her mood had been a combination of temper at being forced into a situation that was a roadblock on her highway to success and frustration at the words her party-time sister had tossed at her about her lack of any life beyond the corporate walls.

Quin smoothed the frown on her brow. "What are you thinking?" he asked deeply.

Caprice focused on him instead of the memories she had deliberately slammed into the back room of her mind. "About what you said. About what Silke said just before we all left home. I don't see how I can change. At least, not in this arena. It is a kind of war. This . . ." She fingered the collar of her blouse. ". . . is my armor. But I honestly don't know how to change it and still do the job I can do. I really don't believe I'd be taken seriously. The corporate ladder is a slippery place. One sign of weakness and there is always someone there waiting to give you a shove into oblivion."

"So you go to war every day for that kind of cause?" His brows rose. "That strikes me as futile as my own campaigning days," he stated bluntly, watching her face.

Caprice frowned again, this time deeper, longer. "I hadn't thought of it that way before."

Quin pulled back before he pushed more than he already had. He respected her mind too much to force change on her. But he also cared too much to sit back while she willfully destroyed the best part of herself. "Don't make your changes, as I did." He turned on the car. "Some things aren't better late than never."

Caprice said little as he guided the car out of the lot and into the early evening traffic. She didn't try to dismiss his words. She had come to value his judgment over the weeks they had spent together. He saw more clearly than most, reducing things, reactions, and people to their barest essentials. He had no patience with excuses or posturing. Yet he had infinite patience for anything or anyone who touched his mind or his emotions. Those he didn't show, except to her, but they existed, as wild and as free as he was.

She envied him that freedom of thought, of choice, she realized suddenly. Her whole life, by her selection, had a structure. She had always thought it kept her safe. It had never occurred to her that it also kept her caged. Was that what Silke had tried to tell her without saying the words? And her mother with her bizarre plan for her and her sisters' redemption?

But she had been content, she argued silently. She frowned more deeply than ever. Not content maybe, but at peace. No, not that either. Set. She tasted the word, finding it bitter when it should have satisfied.

"If I didn't do this, I don't know what I would do," she said slowly as she turned her head to look at Quin. Caught with her own discoveries, she missed the tension in his body. "I didn't want to give up this year. I was the last one to agree, and then I did it only because the rest of my sisters were going to agree." She smiled grimly. "Not a very nice reaction for my parents or even nice feelings to have for my sisters when all any of the three of them has ever done was try to love me."

He heard the pain in her voice, the groping for something to hang on to. She needed him. The feeling was a warmth that fed even as it commanded he give. "You loved them back. Especially Silke," he pointed out.

"I don't know if I did love her, at least not until the last two nights. Oh, I pulled her into the yard that first night when she almost got caught by the police. I had seen her from the window of the rec room. That red hair of hers had caught the street light. I thought she was trying to break into the 'home.' I had some vague idea of being a hero by stopping her. So I sneaked out into the yard, hid behind a tree, and waited." She relived the memory, the feel, the sound of that night. "She looked so hungry. We had just eaten. Lorraine had always insisted that the food be more than institutional fare, so we had had fried chicken, gravy, potatoes, two vegetables, and lemon meringue pie for dessert. I felt guilty. Standing there in the dark, looking at how thin Silke seemed, I felt like I had too much. I almost went back inside. Then I saw the police cruiser. I didn't think. I just reacted, and that had nothing at all to do with Silke. It was my own past that made me grab her hand and yank her through the gate and hide her in the bushes. I hated law enforcement people back then. They took people away. It was us against them." She laughed shortly.

"You loved her later."

She shook her head, her eyes sad. "No. If I had, I would have realized that she wasn't the lush we all thought her. I never asked her. I was so busy with my life, I never gave her or the others a thought. But Silke did. She saw what I should have seen."

"Now, who's being too hard on themselves?"

She blinked, surprised at the quick rebuttal.

"You were a child for part of that time, with problems of your own. I remember that age."

She touched his thigh. His hand immediately covered hers, holding it tight. "My parents tried to get help for all of us. Leora and Noelle took to having a counselor, but Silke and I fought it. Probably the age difference, I suppose. Nothing helped. But talking to you does."

He lifted her fingers to his lips as he stopped the car in the slot allotted to the penthouse suite of the hotel. "I'm glad. You've helped me as well."

"The past isn't so bad if it's shared."

"If it's shared with the right person."

Caprice smiled faintly. "On the surface neither of us should be the right person for the other."

He touched her cheek, stroking the velvet flesh before wrapping his hand around her neck to draw her close. "Masks only."

"Yes," she sighed, offering her lips for his kiss. "But not with each other," she added just before he took possession of her lips.

The rain drizzled irritably onto the city, lightning showing its temper with the world, signaling a storm to come. The man hunched against the rain as he stepped out of the cab and hurried under the shelter of the awning stretched across the entrance of the hotel. He hadn't much time. The wolves were closing with every step. Every avenue of escape had been exhausted, and unless this old tie, a distant debt owed, was remembered, he hadn't a snowball's chance in hell of getting home.

He paused, searching the lobby for the house phones. When he spotted them, he moved casually toward them as though his life didn't depend on making a connection with the one man with enough courage, connections, and power to help him. He should be safe for a few hours until his contact decided he had given those who would kill him the slip. Double cross. Occupational hazard.

Quin stepped out of the shower, pulled a towel from the warming cabinet, and turned as Caprice followed him. He spread the white velour, silently inviting her to curl into its warmth.

"You have a thing about taking care of me," she murmured as he wrapped her up.

"I like doing things for you. I've never cared with any of my other women." He felt her tension despite the thickness of the fabric between his hands and her skin. "Don't."

She shook her head, her smile trying to survive the flash of pain in her eyes. "I shouldn't care. I don't have the right. And you don't use them against me."

He pulled her close, denying her freedom to lift her arms free of the towel. "You do have the right. As I do. I don't want to think of the men who have held you."

She sighed deeply. "There were only two."

"And they meant something to you or you wouldn't have shared yourself with them."

"Neither of them was you."

"Am I so different?"

"You know you are. The first time I saw you, you fascinated me. Then we talked and, suddenly, I felt the danger that surrounded you like an invisible cloak. I wanted nothing more than to escape. You were more man than I had ever known, and I felt less a woman than I had ever been. It was unnerving, disturbing, and frightening. So I ran."

"And I chased you."

"Caught me."

He shook his head. "I did. Then I realized I didn't want you that way. Suddenly, it mattered that I had tricked you with your own body, used my skill to steal when I had promised myself I never would again."

"You made me choose . . ."

Before she could finish speaking the phone rang. Quin glanced over his shoulder to the half-closed bathroom door. "Are you expecting any calls?"

"No. You?"

"No." He dropped a quick kiss on her lips, then moved away. Caprice rewound the towel and followed just in time to hear the faintest hint of surprise in his voice. If she hadn't begun to read his reactions well, she would even have missed that.

"Where are you?" he demanded tersely. Quin listened, his eyes sharp, alert as he stared beyond Caprice. "Your decision stinks, Rolf. You could have brought them right down on my head and you know it. Can the excuses. Damn it! Don't remind me of what I owe." He listened again, a glare destroying the implacable expression. "All right I understand the importance. I don't like being set up and I won't forget." He paused, then nodded decisively. "I'll see what I can do. Find a hole and crawl in. Give me two hours." He hung up without saying good-bye.

Caprice stared at him, seeing the stranger she had seen only twice before. This was the man of the past, the mercenary, the hired mind, the hired gun, the hired skill. "Who is he?" she asked softly, going to stand in front of him. She touched his arm, the ridges of tissue beneath her fingers as familiar now as her own smooth skin.

Quin focused on her worried face. "Someone I know in a hell of a lot of trouble," he said flatly.

"You're going to help him."

He heard the question she didn't ask. "If I don't, he dies. Betrayed by those he trusted. Damn fool. He knows better."

"Tell me how I can help. If I can help."

He stilled, his gaze conveying his shock. "What are you talking about?"

"We're a pair. This doesn't sound like an easy situation. I don't know a thing about your kind of life, but if I can help you, I want to." She spread her hands, wondering if he understood the need she had to be with him. In all the weeks of passion, neither of them had really addressed the future. It was as though, by mutual consent, they had decided it didn't apply.

"It's too dangerous."

"I didn't think it would be anything else."

He searched her face, seeing nothing but her determination to be there for him reflected in her steady look. "Warrior maid," he muttered under his breath.

She smiled faintly, becoming accustomed to the description he used for her when she had thrown him off balance. "If you were tame, I wouldn't have to be," she replied, stepping close enough to brush his bare chest with her towel-covered breasts.

Quin caught her hips in his hands, holding her, unknowingly digging his fingers gently into her. "I don't want you involved." He shook his head when she would have interrupted. "For your protection, not because I wouldn't want you at my side. Trained, I would trust you with my life." He had never told anyone that, and yet, in that moment, he knew it was true. Had she been a comrade in arms, he would have trusted her to die rather than betray him. Her courage was in her commitment. Her strength was in the experiences that had shaped her.

Caprice felt the slow slide of tears on her face. "No one has ever given me a greater compliment," she murmured huskily.

He bent his head over her, his lips a kiss away. "I meant it," he replied deeply.

She touched his cheek. "I know." She closed her eyes for one second, then opened them. "I'm glad we're together."

Quin smiled without restraint, accepting what would have been from another only a faint compliment, but with Caprice one step closer to a commitment. "So am I," he replied before he took her lips in the kiss that was made to link them in the world they had created.

Nine

Quin hung up the phone, aware of Caprice sitting in the chair across from him. She had said nothing through the long series of overseas conversations, but her eyes had followed every movement he had made, every mask he had put on to play the game of life over death. He had hoped she would never know firsthand the experiences that had shaped him. He should have known hoping was a risk for fools.

"Is it done?" Caprice asked softly when Quin continued to stare at her without speaking. "Have you found him a safe place?"

"Yes," he admitted with a sigh. "Or at least as safe as one can be who is newly retired. He carries too much information to be really safe for a while until those who rule his world learn of his absence and readjust the flow of power and information."

"Why did he come to you?" she risked asking.

Quin glanced at his watch, more to give himself a chance to consider his answer than to check the time. He still had a little less than a half hour before he could contact Rolf. "He is the last of the original four."

Caprice's brows rose in surprise. "I thought you said they were all killed."

"I thought they had been. But Rolf was always an elusive fox. He had made his plans to disappear. Like me, he had seen that the new leader was not someone he could follow or trust. So he died."

Thinking that over for a moment, Caprice finally nodded. "The easiest way." She looked at him, realizing even more about this man who could command passion as easily as he commanded men. "You've done that too, haven't you?"

"Yes." He rose to walk to the window, standing just enough to one side so that his body was not a target. The night had gathered around the city while he had maneuvered for the high stakes that had once been the only existence he had known. "Three times I have begun again."

Her own experiences fresh in mind and body of trying to build a new life, cut adrift from all she had known, Caprice understood just how difficult each change had been. "Do you get to take anything with you?"

He turned, facing her, leaning back against the wall. "No. Anything, no matter how small, can be a clue in the right hands. It is a complete break. Different name, appearances, habits, work, friends, living arrangements, pastimes." He spread his hands in a gesture foreign to the image he presented. For one moment, the man he had been born seeped into this life. "So you see before you the embodiment of a lie."

Caprice heard the bitter acceptance beneath the blunt announcement. Without thinking, knowing only that she could not bear to hear his pain, much less see it, she went to him, wrapping her arms around his waist. His came up to claim her. "You are no lie. I do not care what name you were born with. I do not care what habits you've learned to match the identity you now have."

She searched his face, seeing the harshness that tried to reject her complete acceptance. "I do care that you live. The man you are, the part of you that matters to me hasn't changed. If you had plastic surgery so perfectly that none of this remained . . ." She touched his cheek, the strong line of his jaw, his brow. "If you spoke in a language I didn't understand, did work I had never seen, lived in a world I have never known, I would still know you."

"How?"

She smiled, realizing suddenly just how much she had given this man. Herself. All of her needs, her wants, her hopes, and her dreams lay in his hands. She could have been a child to blurt out her discovery. She knew better. Instead, she shielded the love she felt pouring into her soul from where it had lain unearthed in her heart. She held the emotion close to the core of strength where it was her treasure rather than his burden.

"Because you can and did, I'm sure, change the superficial things, but you didn't change your heart, your soul. You've shown me those whether you meant to or not. That is how I would know you. If I were blind, deaf, or mute, I would remember the feel of your thoughts, the taste of your gentleness, the challenge of your boldness. That you cannot hide."

Many things had he faced—death, life, hatred, and cruelty. But her words, soft, sure, and infinite in their acceptance, struck to the center of his body, chaining him in such a way that he would never know freedom. For the first time in his life, he looked into a cage and found it less than a trap to enslave, to destroy. He looked deep into her eyes and saw the love that she held silent. He read, too, her determination not to be a weight about his neck. She would walk beside him, this woman he had chosen and who had been decreed by a more powerful hand than his to belong to him.

"Live with me," he whispered, the words driven from him by his need to bring her into the golden mesh with him. "Come with me now or when your year is done."

Caprice held his words close to her heart, feeding the mute love she bore him. "You may not want me then."

He shook his head, understanding her fear as he always had. Her life was the opposite pole of his own. The choice had to be hers. He knew what he could offer and what was beyond his power. "I will want you with my last thought of this earth. I will carry you into eternity while I wait to breathe again."

His eyes held truth. His arms promised the same. She wanted to believe him and she did. But she also knew herself. He could live his life of changes. But for her, it was a world that had too many memories of dark night escapes, unstable lives, frightening whispers of anxiety to steal what little peace there was to be found. She had not his strength regardless of his belief in the warrior maid. She had not his skill at camouflage either. The first she might have been able to offer out of love. But the last? She was a liability that could easily cost him his life.

"No." The swift flash of anger and hard determination neither frightened nor deterred her from her choice. "I will stay with you here. For as long as you wish. But I will not join you. I can't."

"The material things that you choose for your secure world are more important after all," he stated, his eyes narrowed in temper and disbelief. Every instinct fought her denial of what could be theirs. He had been so certain that she realized her own strength, that these weeks with him had taught her that the future was anything she wished to make of it. "You speak pretty words, but you hold to things that can be destroyed so easily."

She covered his mouth with her palm. The pain of his words was great, but the hurtful force that drove him to speak them was greater. "Think, my poet. Be a realist for a moment. Can I walk the maze of life and death of your world without danger to you? Have I the skill, or had you thought to protect me as a child and probably risk yourself in the process? Has anything I have done or said led you to believe that I would accept such a sacrifice? As for the things, I need structure. I can't move with your ease from one identity to another. I am afraid. Simple to say. But almost impossible to counter. My fear is my rock to carry. I would not wish it to be yours."

"How can it not be? I have known you. You let me in. We are linked. You cannot wish that away."

"I don't. But I won't have your blood on my hands either."

Impasse. A word he hated. Frustration tore at him, a taunting voice to tease him with what he could not have and wanted desperately. "I won't give you up. I told you that from the beginning."

"And I won't risk you with my ignorance and fear," she returned just as strongly.

He searched her eyes, finding no weakness, no toehold to breach her defenses. He pulled her hard against him, the only avenue left to reach her. Passion. No longer a beast tamed to his hand, the emotion lifted its head, breathing the fire of his anger and frustration. His features tightened into a mass of suffering and desperate need. His strength doubled, slipping past the restraint on which he had always counted.

Caprice stilled, feeling as though he had just snatched her off firm ground and held her over a bottomless pit. Destruction was a heartbeat away. And it wouldn't be just her destruction. It would be his as well. She lifted her hand, her eyes filling with tears when he flinched, the rage in him intensifying.

"Please don't do this to us," she whispered, her voice as soft as the gentlest of touches.

"Damn that word to hell," he said roughly, his hands sinking into her, marking her even as he stood looming over her. "You denied us for old fears that we could have fought together. I gave you everything."

The tears overflowed. "You will hate yourself for this. The poet will destroy himself. Please, Quin, do not." Caprice held his gaze despite the blurring of her tears. There was no way she could fight him if he truly decided to take her in anger. Her love as much as his superior strength was an unbreakable chain. "Please," she murmured one last time, then laid her head against his heart. If he was bent on destroying them, she would not look. She couldn't bear to see the hatred for himself that would be in his eyes when his rage had burned them both to ashes.

Quin stared at her head pressed against his chest. For one moment, every primitive instinct he possessed demanded action. She loved him. He would make her admit it. Sliding his fingers through her hair, he tipped her head back. Her eyes were closed, silent grief slipping through her lashes to dampen his shirt and paint her skin with crystalline highlights. He shuddered deeply. Those tears reminded him of the night she had cried for him. His fingers gentled, cradling her head rather than imprisoning it. He sighed deeply, audibly, the rage to possess dying.

"Open your eyes," he commanded finally, roughly.

Even locked in her dark world, Caprice felt the changes in him. She lifted her lashes, looking straight into the silver depths of his eyes.

"I would not have been able to hurt you physically. I wanted to. But I wouldn't have been able to do it."

Caprice lifted her free arm, curling it around his neck. "I know. But both of us would have remembered."

"That's still true. You will remember what I almost did."

She shook her head. "No. I will remember that because I asked it of you, you went against your own needs and instincts for mine. That will never be a bad memory, only a good one."

"I don't want to be a memory."

"I won't be a risk to you. And I would be. No amount of rationalizing on your part will change that. I will always be a chink in your armor."

"I can live with it."

"I can't."

"Won't."

She covered his lips with her palm. "Can't. I will let you go. I will live alone even if I take another man to my bed. You will always live in my heart. I will not see you die in my arms."

He studied her face, realizing that never had the warrior maid been more in evidence. She was confronting an enemy without one weapon to defend herself and still she dared to fight. "You cannot change destiny."

Her smile was painful, but she managed it. "I can try." She stepped back, out of his arms, away from his warmth. "Now, go, make your call. Your man waits for you."

"This is not the end."

"I know."

He looked at her for one more moment. He spoke of one thing, but she meant another. Which of them would win?

Quin scanned the packed bar in the heart of the wrong side of town. The crowd could have been a product of any city. Only the language marked the location. The air was filled with smoke, distrust, anger, and a braggart's pride. He strolled through the jammed space, his body flowing easily from one step to the next. He fitted in with his well-worn jeans, shirt that had seen better days, and scuffed boots. Instead of the expensive watch he normally wore, his had a sweat-stained leather band that had seen a lot of use. Even the crystal of the face was scratched and chipped. Props. He knew them well and used them with skill. He stepped up to the bar, his eyes on the rotund man behind the scarred counter.

"Beer," he ordered in a muted drawl. Rolf sat beside him, but he paid no attention. His beer came. He took a slug, his eyes on the mirror in front of him. One of the pool tables in the back corner of the room was his target. He had finished little more than half of his bottle when the final shots were sunk. He turned around and sauntered over. "Wanta game?" he asked the man remaining beside the table.

He looked up, scowling. "No way, man. I just lost all my damn money. You need to pick yourself a better sucker." He slammed down his cue and stalked off.

"I'll give you a game."

Quin glanced at Rolf as though sizing him up, then gave a short nod. "Quarter a point?"

Rolf grimaced, then took a swig out of his own beer. "All right by me." He moved to the rack to select a cue stick. "Flip for break?"

Quin dug int his pocket for two quarters. He flipped one, calling his choice.

Rolf shrugged when Quin won. "Your break."

Quin fed the two quarters into the table and racked the balls. "Eight ball?"

"Better than nothing."

Less than ten minutes later, Quin left the bar without a backward look. He had a few more dollars in his pocket than he had gone in with and Rolf had his arrangements for exiting the country in hand. Quin should have felt a sense of completion. Instead, his instincts were more strongly on alert than ever. His gaze scanned the area around the bar as he entered the lot where he had parked the nondescript car he had used. Nothing looked out of place, no man loitering where he shouldn't be. But he couldn't shake the feeling that he was walking or had walked into a trap. Even when he got into the car, he was tense, waiting for an ambush.

Worried, his brow furrowed as he drove, he searched his rear-view mirror for any signs of a tail. The fact that there was none wasn't reassuring. Instead of going straight back to the hotel, he wound his way through the city, parking the car on a street still teeming with life. Getting out, he wandered down the sidewalk, stopping occasionally as though he had all the time in the world. Finally, satisfied that no one was interested in him, he slipped into a store, waited until he had the chance, then left through the back. The alley gave cover and he used it, coming out three streets away. He hailed a cab, took it to another area of the city, and used the same precautions before he decided it was safe to go back to the hotel where Caprice waited.

"We lost him."

"I told you that he was the best. Did you put the homing device in the car?"

"He ditched it.

"Your man couldn't follow?"

"Lost within two miles of the bar."

"Incompetents."

The subordinate nodded unhappily. His boss was not a forgiving man and this assignment was more critical than most. "What would you like me to do?"

"Besides collect a new team?" He smiled grimly, his fingers stroking the gun lying on the desk beside his left hand. "I will allow you one more chance. Find the woman."

"We're working on it."

"Work harder."

The hireling swallowed convulsively.

"I see you understand, my friend. There will be no more mistakes. Do I make myself clear? I have my orders. You have yours."

"I understand." He rose, eager to escape.

"Bring her to me when you get her."

He glanced over his shoulder, startled at the request. "Here?" he repeated.

"Here. I have a score to settle with Rom. More than this plum assignment our bosses have seen fit to offer this renegade gypsy." His fingers curled around the gun as he leaned forward. The light shone on his face, highlighting the wicked slash down his right cheek. "I will destroy anyone who deprives me of my sport."

"I won't forget," the younger man promised before leaving while he could.

Caprice paced the hotel room, alternating between cursing the slow drag of the minutes and praying that Quin would be all right. She hadn't known she could worry about anyone outside her family this much. She looked at the clock on the bedside stand, glaring at the time. He should be back by now. He had promised no more than two hours. She turned and paced back to the window, but didn't pause in front of the closed drapes as he had ordered her not to do. Precautions. She wasn't accustomed to taking them. She felt like she was in a cage of both time and space and only Quin held the keys to freedom.

Suddenly she heard a soft whisper of sound from the outer door. Rushing into the sitting room, she arrived just as Quin shut the door behind him. She didn't think. She simply reacted.

"You're late! Is everything all right?" She didn't wait for an answer as she launched herself into his arms.

Quin caught her close, stunned at the swift glimpse of anxiety he had seen on her face before she buried her head against his shoulder. "I'm fine," he murmured, hardly aware that his body curved protectively over her as his arms tightened. "I told you I would be."

She lifted her head, glaring up at him. "I told *you* I wasn't trained to handle danger well. You took longer than you promised." She touched his face. "Why?" She caught the change of expression in his eyes before he could mask it. "Something's wrong. What is it?"

He shook his head. "Nothing specific."

She studied his face, seeing the uneasiness he wasn't trying to hide from her. "But you feel like there is?"

He sighed deeply. "Yes. I feel a trap," he stated bluntly, curling his arm around her shoulders as he urged her toward the couch.

"What are you going to do?"

"Get you out of harm's way first."

She frowned. "You think they will come here? Whoever they are? Even if they do, they won't bother me."

"You aren't naive and we haven't been hiding the fact we've been seeing each other."

"I'm not the first woman in your life," she pointed out practically. Despite the fact that neither of them had spoken the words, Caprice knew Quin loved her. The women who had shared his past no longer mattered enough for her to avoid mentioning or thinking about them.

He scowled at the reminder. "Don't place yourself with the others. I won't have it." He caught her shoulders and dragged her into his lap. "Take it back."

Her head tipped over his arm, she circled his neck and tugged gently. "Stop growling, my gypsy," she whispered as though the walls had ears. "I don't care about them now that I know you didn't."

He cupped her chin with his scarred fingers. "You are sure?"

"Very."

He brushed her lips lightly, not daring to take what his body really craved. He had a feeling that his past was hurtling down on his present. He didn't want her caught in the middle of the explosive meeting. "Then you will let me get you out of this. As long as they chase me, you are in danger."

"You don't know that 'they' are chasing you."

"I have lived too long not to trust my feelings more than my sight and hearing. The woods are filled with hunters and I am the prey. But you will not be. I promise." He looked deep into her eyes. "Do you believe me?"

She didn't hesitate. "Yes."

"Thank you." He smiled, feeling the first lightening of the

worry that had dogged him since he had begun to sense a trap. "I will make arrangements for you to leave for the island tonight. You will have to leave your things, but I will have others waiting for you."

Caprice frowned. "What do you mean, leave for the island?"

"It is the only place I can reasonably guarantee your safety." Uneasiness returned in a rush as he read the rejection in her eyes. "No."

"What do you mean no? You have said you trust me."

"And I do. But I will break my word if I go. I can't." She pushed at his shoulders, knowing she would not be able to get free unless he allowed it. For one moment, he resisted her efforts, then he released her, his eyes never leaving hers. "Try to understand. This is my world, my life. My family asked something of me, the first something of me. I didn't wish to rip my future apart but I agreed. I can't go back on that. I gave my word."

Quin surged to his feet, frustrated. He understood the power a code of honor had in some people, himself included. Caprice was making the same decision he would have made in the same circumstances, but that didn't make him accept her choice. "You don't know what these people are like."

"No, I don't. But I can guess."

He swung around, pinning her with a steely look. "No, you cannot. I will not paint you the picture of their ugliness. But know this. They will not care if you are a St. James or a woman or innocent of all of this. They will care only about your use to them, dead or alive."

"You have people on your island to protect me?"

Hope blotted out despair for a moment. "Yes. Enough to protect you for as long as necessary."

"People you have trained, perhaps relied on in situations like this?"

"Yes. They are very experienced."

"And if you needed help, you would summon one or a few of them, wouldn't you?"

Quin saw the trap too late to escape with a lie. "Yes," he said, cursing his honesty.

She inclined her head. "I said that you would protect me at the expense of yourself. Even if I could break my word, I would not buy my safety at the expense of yours. If I were at the island, you would not call. You would face your hunters alone, perhaps be brought down. I can't live with that," she stated flatly, a strange curve of tenderness to her lips. "I will take my chances here. If nothing else, you will be forced to bring help to watch over me and that will spill over onto you."

Quin's hands clenched into fists as he faced her choice and knew that he would not be able to argue her out of it. "You say you do not take risks. You lie. You are risking your life for mine."

"It's my choice to make."

Ten

Quin eased out of bed, watching as Caprice shifted restlessly in her sleep. When she didn't awaken, he moved silently out of the room, closing the door soundlessly behind him. He didn't turn on any lights. The darkness was a welcome ally for the thinking he needed to do. No matter how he had argued, Caprice had stood firm. She would not go. And yet his instincts said she was in great danger. Perhaps it was his own emotion that made him see demons where there were none, but he didn't think so. Rolf was the key, yet try as he would he could not believe the man would sell him out without more than just money waiting at the dock. Nor could he find anything in his massive network of contacts to indicate that Rolf had changed from associate to foe. Besides, Rolf simply didn't feel right. No, the danger, wherever its source, did not come from Rolf's direction. Which meant that there was another player, a shadow from a past filled with them. With no name, he was left with a blanket defense that did little more than warn, never protect. No matter how careful, he was dissatisfied with the odds. His decision made, he reached for the phone.

Killian's voice was thick with sleep when he answered.

"Explain to me exactly what kind of surveillance you have on Caprice," Quin commanded without bothering to identify himself.

Killian pushed upright in the bed, glaring at the man he couldn't see. "Damn you. Did you call me at three o'clock in the morning to ask me that? Where are you, as if I need to ask?"

"In Houston. And before you ask, Caprice is in my bed."

Killian scowled. "If I didn't know you better than that and if there weren't a few thousand miles separating us, I'd hand you your head to tuck under your arm for a remark like that."

Disturbed by the irritable voice of her husband, Silke rolled over, blinking groggily. "What's wrong?"

Killian pulled her close to his side, brushing her lips to silence her.

"This is serious," Quin muttered, too aware of Caprice sleeping in the next room.

Killian stiffened. "How bad and who?"

Quin swore graphically. "That's part of the problem. I don't know. It's a feeling right now. The kind that keeps you alive if you heed it and gets you killed if you don't."

"Get her out of there. I'll set it up on my end."

"I tried that. She won't go," he stated flatly. "She gave her word to Lorraine and she's not budging."

Killian's scowl deepened. "That doesn't sound like Caprice. What aren't you telling me?"

"She thinks she's in love with me and she believes that if she goes to the island, I'll keep my men there instead of bringing them here as reinforcements."

"She must have gotten to you if she's figured you that well," Killian murmured. "The prophecy's coming true after all. Even after all these years."

Quin frowned deeply. "Can the prophecy. That kind of thinking can get her killed. You know the type of people we're dealing with. This isn't some story one reads."

"If she's gotten to you, you must know her history by now. Caprice isn't a woman to believe any story. She learned distrust too early to handle the opposite now."

"I didn't call you for a lecture on her or what we are to each other."

In spite of the situation, Killian felt a flash of humor at the irritation he had never heard Quin display. "All right. What did you call for?"

"To tell you not to get upset if Caprice turns up missing in the next few days." Quin leaned back in his chair, staring into the darkness.

Any humor left his eyes and voice at the announcement. "Run that by me again."

"I thought that might get your attention."

"It's doing a lot more than that. Get to the point."

"If Caprice won't go to the island willingly, I'll send her unwillingly," he said simply.

"Kidnap her, you mean," Killian said flatly.

"If you need a name, that one will do."

"I have a better idea. Let me talk to Lorraine and Geoffrey. She'll come home for them."

Quin considered that. The island was a controlled area and therefore safer than anything Killian could provide in Philadelphia. But he would be forcing Caprice into a situation that she had told him she did not want. "You could try it," he agreed slowly.

"You don't think she'll come?"

"I don't know. I can promise you she'll be in a temper when she finds out I have called you."

"Caprice doesn't have one."

Quin laughed shortly. "Ask Silke."

Killian leaned over, switched on the bedside light, and opened the drawer of the table to pull out a pad and pencil. "Give me the number of where you're staying. I'll talk to Lorraine and Geoffrey as soon as we hang up. My bet is that they'll call her the minute they make their decision."

"If she doesn't agree, I'm taking her out of this," Quin warned, his tone making it clear he would brook no interference. "I got her into this. I'll give all of you one chance to get her out. Not for my sake but for hers. After that, all deals are off."

"You sound like I did when Silke was in danger."

"I probably feel like you," Quin muttered. "That damn picture I stole from Silke sure didn't show Caprice in a real light. That woman had a backbone of steel and the stubborn disposition of a mule who is carrying one stick too many on his back," Quin said in disgust, his accent richer than usual.

Killian laughed, his arm tightening around his wife. "These St. James women are a deceptive bunch. Look like one thing to a man and then, the minute he gets them in his arms, they turn into a species no male has ever dealt with."

"At another time, I would appreciate the challenge."

Killian sobered. "I remember that feeling, too," he agreed with a sigh. "Need anything else before I start waking up people?"

"No. Whatever plans are in the works probably aren't of the immediate kind. For someone to want me after all this time and to be able to dig deep enough to trace me here means we're not just dealing with the average hunter."

"That doesn't reassure me."

Quin's grim face wouldn't have either. "There is only one man I can think of with a need this strong."

Killian inhaled sharply, remembering. "Gustaf."

"Yes. If it is he, we have time. He likes his strategies too much and he thinks himself a master of logistics. That may be the only thing that gives us any margin of safety," he stated bluntly before hanging up.

Killian wasted no time in dialing Lorraine and Geoffrey to apprise them of the problem. Explaining Quin's role in the situation was difficult, but he managed it without giving Quin's background away or actually saying that it was because of Quin and his past that Caprice was in danger at all. No matter what the future held for the man who had helped him save Silke's life, he would do nothing to prejudice his chances.

"I am getting too old for these kinds of shocks," Geoffrey muttered. "First Silke and now Caprice. I thought my daughters were fairly ordinary."

Killian grunted noncommittally as he glanced over at the sleek piece of female curled snugly against his side. "I don't think ordinary describes either Silke or Caprice."

Geoffrey sighed deeply. "Perhaps not. But a man can hope. I'll talk to Lorraine about this, but I can guarantee that we will be speaking to Caprice in the next hour. Will you make the arrangements? Call the company pilot and have him fly down to pick her up. I suppose you will have a man on the plane."

"I intend to go myself."

"Good," Geoffrey agreed in relief.

"Quin doesn't think she'll return," Killian warned.

Geoffrey thought that over. "She is involved with this man, really involved?"

"I think so," Killian murmured, telling the truth without putting too much emphasis on it.

"The kind of man better as a friend than an enemy?"

"Yes."

"He is trustworthy?"

"More than I can tell you."

Geoffrey was no fool, and their relationship, both professional and personal, had spanned a number of years. "A man with shadows."

"Are there any with any kind of success or power who don't have them?"

"No. Perhaps it is better. Caprice would not care for a man who had milk in his veins."

Killian laughed. "No, that I think we can all definitely guarantee."

"I'll let you know when she will be ready."

Killian didn't bother reminding him again that there was a very good chance that Caprice wouldn't agree. He had a feeling, not unlike Quin's, that Caprice wasn't leaving by anything less than force.

When Killian hung up from Geoffrey, he made three other calls arranging for the St. James Lear to be preflighted, the pilot to be waiting, and his office to be notified of his impending departure. With all that could be done finished until Geoffrey called back, he settled himself comfortably in the bed to wait. Killian leaned over and brushed his lips against Silke's waiting mouth. So far she had asked no questions. But because they no longer had secrets between them, questions weren't necessary. He would tell her the truth and she knew and accepted that.

"Do you have a picture of Caprice?"

Silke frowned at the question, her golden eyes more alert than her languid movements indicated. She had heard enough of what was going on to know that Caprice was in danger. There were a dozen useless questions she could have asked, but she voiced none of them. She knew her husband, read the worry in his eyes and the tension of the enforced wait in his body. If he needed a diversion, she would play along with him.

"I did have one, in my wallet. But it got lost that afternoon in the garage when Eric tried to kill me."

"It didn't get lost. Quin took it."

She frowned. "Why? If he had asked, I would have had a copy made."

"And asked a lot of questions in the process."

"Probably."

"He wouldn't have answered."

Remembering the man who had come to her aid at Killian's request, Silke had to agree. "I still don't understand."

"About fifteen years ago, Quin and I ended up as associates in the loosest sense of the word. In the process we stumbled into a society that had a few rather interesting tricks up its collective sleeve. When we finished what we had come to do, we took a short R and R detour in that same society. Although to be perfectly honest, my detour was considerably shorter than his." He grunted as Silke prodded him with a finger to stop taking so long to get to the point. "You have no patience," he complained, imprisoning her hand before she could jab him again.

"You should know that by now," she reminded him.

"We've only been married a little over a month."

"Some things don't need time," she pointed out smugly. "Now, get on with your story."

"Quin and I ran into a man who was intent on reading our futures for us. I don't believe in that kind of thing, but Quin, with his gypsy background, does. He listened. It sounded like a lot of double-talk to me, but he tucked the words away in that computer brain of his and waited."

Silke frowned. "For what?"

"A sister who wasn't a sister. A woman who would slay dragons and light the darkness of one man's hell."

"Caprice? No wonder he sounded so surprised when I said I had an adopted sister." She paused, thinking that over.

"He went after her, didn't he? I remember noticing at the wedding that he seemed to watch her a lot, but men usually do until she freezes them out."

"She didn't freeze him out."

She smiled at that, imagining the battle between two strong-willed and course-set people. "I almost wish I could be a fly on the wall to hear what they say when Caprice realizes Quin called for reinforcements. My sister definitely doesn't like anyone pushing her into making choices or changes. She's got a temper that puts mine to shame."

Killian's brows rose. "I haven't seen any evidence of it, or heard any for that matter."

Silke laughed softly. "I think you are going to get some first-hand experience if I know her at all. In fact, I think I'll let you answer the phone from now until the time you leave, if you leave."

Killian eyed her suspiciously. "Is it really that bad?"

"You said you had dossiers on all of us. Didn't you read Caprice's?"

"She was thirteen when she bashed that man over the head with a broom."

"And wrecked his store. And poured paint down his male parts, oil paint no less, so that he had to have it taken off at the emergency room."

"Making a few suggestive remarks to a girl of thirteen is a lot different from dealing with a woman of almost thirty."

Silke patted his arm. "I'll still let you explain the difference to my sister. I'll just stand on the sidelines with the first-aid kit."

"You did what?" Caprice demanded softly, staring at Quin as though she had never seen him before.

Quin reached out to pull her into his arms. She dodged out of his hold, despite the sheet she had wound around her body against the coolness of the air-conditioned room. Jamming his hands in the pocket of his jeans, he studied her angry expression. "I called Killian to tell him about the situation we're in."

"You aren't even sure there is a situation." Caprice blew the hair out of her eyes. There were much better ways to have a confrontation of this magnitude besides standing in one's birthday suit, wrapped in a sheet after having been awakened in the middle of the night with a kiss that had promised passion rather than an announcement of betrayal.

"I'm not willing to take the chance."

Caprice's fingers clenched around the sheet, her temper slipping another notch. "You aren't willing," she began dangerously. Before she could open her mouth for another word the phone rang. She swung around, glaring at it as though it were a mortal enemy.

Quin's expression showed no remorse. He would do what he had done and more to keep her safe. "That will be your parents."

"Worried sick, no doubt."

He inclined his head, no apology in his eyes. "They wouldn't have been if you had agreed to let me take you out of the line of fire."

She stamped her foot, the effect lost because of the thick carpet and her lack of shoes. "I keep telling you there is no fire for certain. I'll agree to your instincts. I'll even take precautions, all the extra ones you want. But I won't leave, either to go home or to your island. And I won't be forced into either course by any of you." She stalked, or tried to, to the phone, stumbling on the trailing ends of the covers and cursing when the top slipped too much for her liking. A knot of material in one hand, she grabbed for the phone with the other.

"Yes, Mother," she said, trying to be pleasant despite her gritted teeth. She turned to glare at Quin as she listened to her mother rescind her wish for her to stay in Houston. "No, Mother," she said as gently as she could manage. "I'm not coming home."

"Be reasonable, my dear. I never intended this. If anything happens to you, it will be my fault," Lorraine pleaded.

"No, it won't," Caprice disagreed strongly. "I'm a grown woman and I am responsible for my life. I haven't lived it well until now. You were right about that. But I think I have my priorities right, or at least they're getting there. I gave my word to stay and I'm keeping it."

"But it's dangerous."

"Quin thinks it's dangerous," she corrected. "You and Father provided me with a watchdog. And we will be careful."

Lorraine sighed deeply, unhappily. "I can't make you come home," she admitted tiredly. "But I wish I could."

Listening to the defeat in her mother's voice, Caprice tightened her fingers on the phone. For one second she almost gave in to the emotional pressure. Then she looked at the man she loved and knew, whatever risks she was running, his were multiplied more than she could count. Her anger cooled. She couldn't leave him even to save herself. She had spent years holding herself aloof from others, protecting herself at their expense. She just couldn't do it anymore.

"I love you, Mother. I love you both," she said gently before she carefully replaced the receiver.

Quin read the bone-deep determination in Caprice's eyes. He had hoped and known, even as he was hoping, that she would not go. Because of her decision, there was no other course. He moved to stand in front of her, his eyes searching hers. The anger was gone from the smoky emerald depths. He touched her cheek.

"I had to try to protect you," he murmured, for the first time in his life offering an explanation for his actions.

She nodded. "I know. I would have done the same."

"You aren't angry."

"Not now." She smiled faintly. "But I'm sure I will be again."

She took the step that was needed to walk into his arms. They were waiting to receive her. The sheet slid mutely to the floor between them. For now, no barriers were needed. What was left of the night called, whispering of secrets more important than plans.

He sat in a pool of golden light, his pen moving lazily across the sheet of paper. The smile on his face promised the dreams of the damned for the man whose name rose out of the first line of writing. His plans were laid. Finally, retribution was at hand. He reached up, stroking the slash that had stolen his looks. He did not forget, and he had never learned to forgive. The gypsy was his.

Eleven

"You're crazy," Killian said bluntly. "You expect me to agree to this? It's my man down there watching her. How do you plan on taking him out? Or is this one of those need-to-know situations?"

Quin leaned back in his chair. If anyone had been watching, he would have looked relaxed. The truth was far different. He was dicing with death, but this time the stakes were more important than his life. "I won't hurt your field man. Just put him out of the

picture for the time it takes to slip Caprice out of the country. I
didn't want you to worry when she showed up missing. Nor did
I want her family to be upset."

"She's not going to forgive you for this."

"I don't care."

Killian swore when he heard the mild words that should have
contained at least a little concern. Quin calm was Quin more dangerous than any man he had ever known. Quin never invited vio-
lence, not like so many of their kind. He neither sought trouble
nor worried about it beyond the most logical of precautions. He
had a fatalistic expectance of his own mortality that was stunning.
But not, apparently, where Caprice was concerned.

"You know the kind of chance you're taking by sending her to
the island. Even if Gustaf is behind this plot, you don't know from
which direction the danger is coming. Your people haven't even
been able to come up with anything to pinpoint his location. All
they know is that he is in the country. The minute you send Caprice
out on your plane, not only have you effectively grounded yourself
unless you want to risk chartering unknown equipment, but you
have left a trail straight to your lair."

"As long as Caprice is safe, it makes no difference."

Frustrated, Killian thrust his fingers into his hair as he tried to
think of a way to make Quin change his mind. He didn't doubt
Quin would handle his plans with finesse and emotionless precision. He just didn't like the feel of what was going on. Every
instinct screamed setup.

"Damn it!" he finally said sharply. He paused, his own instincts
in overdrive.

Quin glanced at his watch. It was nearly time to pick Caprice
up at her job. He had spent all morning making his arrangements.
Every piece was in place to whisk Caprice to safety before the
night was done.

"I'm coming down there."

"You have a wife."

"And you wouldn't ask for help."

"I do not believe it is necessary. Gustaf is an old enemy. He
may win, but the odds are more in my favor than his as long as
Caprice is not a player."

Killian absorbed that. To his knowledge Quin had never made

any commitment to anyone. To a job, yes. But another person, man or woman, no. He paid his debts but never more. "Then take her out of there," he agreed with a sigh that stretched to his soul. "I'll cover here."

Quin felt the tension flow from him. He would have taken Caprice no matter what Killian had said. But it was better this way. He did not wish to hurt this man, but he would have dared even that for Caprice.

"I'm still coming," Killian added.

"There is no debt," he murmured, his lips curving into a smile no one but he noticed.

"Your opinion. Not mine and definitely not Silke's. You helped me save her life."

"I asked a few questions and used a few hours watching a man you handled with ease," he returned.

"You're wasting your time."

Quin sighed. "I know. You always were stubborn."

Killian laughed shortly. "Among other things."

"She will be gone before you get here."

"I didn't think otherwise."

Neither man bothered with the standard phrases to break the connection. Plans had been made. No more was needed.

Quin got to his feet, contemplating those next few hours. The drug he intended to use on Caprice was nothing more than a sleeping pill that would slip easily into her drink at dinner. His pilot was standing ready to fly her straight to the island, where his people were waiting, prepared to withstand a siege that probably would not come as long as he stayed in the open. That was one variable that held the most danger. If he went underground to protect his back, Caprice's danger magnified. She was the bargaining chip, and somehow Gustaf had discovered her value. He stopped at the window, staring down at the street while staying out of sight range. A second later a knock at the outer door of the suite stole his attention. It was a bellman with a note. Quin closed the door, then slit the envelope.

So the gypsy called Randall Quinlan is hunting a mate. I congratulate you, my friend. Your taste, as always, is impeccable. However, there is still the outstanding matter between us. I have even enclosed directions for where I will be to save your so valuable time in hunting for me. By the way, don't bother contacting your woman. She is still at her office and will remain so unless you fail to meet me.

Gustaf

Quin's eyes glittered with rage as he raised his head. Threats had never gained more than his contempt. But this one had the power of a gut shot. In trying to give Caprice a choice, he might just have stolen precious hours from her life. He had no choice. He had to meet Gustaf. The only good thing was that the man would need time to mount a kidnapping. His own plans were already set. He needed to stall Gustaf just long enough to get Caprice out of the country. For now, she was as safe as she could be in her office, with Killian's man watching her.

"Ms. St. James, this just came for you," the runner murmured nervously as she stood poised in the doorway of Caprice's office.

Caprice looked up from the contract she had been studying, focusing on the girl's anxious face. "For me? Interoffice?"

She shook her head. "No. Outside. There is a man waiting for you downstairs."

Caprice frowned as she looked at her watch. Quin was early. He had said to be ready no later than five-thirty. It was just barely past four. The idea of his changing plans didn't match the man she loved. Something was wrong. "What did he look like?"

The girl shrugged. "Real tall. Blond. Handsome."

Caprice relaxed slightly. At least he was safe. Collecting the papers, she stuffed them into her briefcase and slipped her suit jacket off the back of her chair. She rose, shrugged into it, and got her handbag out of the bottom drawer. With all the overtime she had been putting in, at least she didn't have to worry about shorting the company, she decided as she tapped on her superior's door to let him know she was leaving for the day.

"You always were a prompt son of hell," Gustaf said softly, staring at the man he hated more than any other in the world.

Quin entered the room, ignoring the gentle click of the lock being turned on the door behind him. "You're wasting your time."

Gustaf leaned back in his chair, shaking his head, his eyes amused, and satisfied. "You know until this moment I wasn't sure just how important she was to you."

Shrugging, Quin took the chair that faced the desk. Danger waited in the open, outside the door. But not here. Gustaf wanted his instant of triumph, but he wasn't getting it just yet. "I don't spill innocent blood," he said mildly, almost indifferently. He could not capitulate too soon or Gustaf would smell a stall. "I never have."

"Honor? You always have managed to make the rest of us look less than men with that code of yours." Gustaf fingered the scar on his cheek.

Quin said nothing.

Gustaf glanced at his watch, his smile deepening just as the phone rang. He nodded toward it. "Answer it. She will want to speak to you."

Quin stared into those laughing eyes, eyes that flirted with madness, and knew that despite the precautions both Killian and he had taken since the moment he had suspected trouble, Caprice was no longer safe. He didn't waste time with threats. He simply obeyed the order.

"Quin?"

"I'm here, Caprice."

"And she's not," a rough voice said before the connection was broken.

Quin replaced the receiver, not one flicker of expression to betray the rage bottled up inside of him. She had sounded more angry than afraid. But that state of affairs could change in a heartbeat with one word from the man across from him.

"Nothing to say."

Quin shrugged. "I will say something when words matter."

Gustaf tipped back his head, laughing in honest amusement. "My friend, I truly wish you had stayed with me all those years ago. I would not have trusted you, but I would have enjoyed having you as a partner."

Quin waited.

Gustaf sobered, studying him as though he were a new species, not a man he had hated for nearly twenty years. "Some people I do business with on occasion would like to hire your services. But

I, knowing the contrary son of Satan you can be about this kind of assignment, decided to tip the scales in our favor."

Still Quin waited.

Gustaf picked up a single sheet of paper with a small picture attached and slid it across the desk. He waited a second while Quin gave it no more than a cursory glance. "I shall give you your woman, maybe untouched, maybe not. But she will live if this man is no longer alive to cause my associates problems. You have a week, seven long days for your woman to share with me," he added in case Quin had not understood the situation in its entirety.

Fury filled Quin's mind, for one instant almost erasing all logical thought. Gustaf would take great pleasure in breaking Caprice in the most soul-destroying way he knew, and the man knew a lot about the dark cruelties that humans had developed through the ages. It took every ounce of training he possessed to keep the rage from his expression and his muscles relaxed. He rose without speaking and headed for the locked door.

Gustaf's breath inhaled in a hiss of frustration over the action he had not expected. He had been so certain he had found a weakness in the man he hated. "I will have your answer."

"You will have nothing with a deal like that," Quin said without breaking stride or even looking over his shoulder. Caprice's life hung suspended from the string of his skill and his ability to outplay Gustaf in this game.

Gustaf let him reach the door, his hands clenched on the arms of his chair as he watched Quin's back. "If I guarantee her safety?"

Quin reached for the knob.

Gustaf's eyes narrowed with temper. His associates paid too well to make him forget completely that he had to get Quin's agreement. "I give my word."

Quin froze, letting the silence demand what he would have.

"I will oversee her personally but only for this night. Finish the job tonight and I shall return her to you untouched."

Quin turned then, judging the truth and the lie. He knew what the job in question meant both to the man sitting before him and to the party that had hired him to make the contact. He also knew the price of failure. "Make the call," he commanded softly, his voice cool enough to douse the fires of hell.

Gustaf glared at him. "You do not trust me."

Quin's gaze moved to the scar on Gustaf's cheek. The other man flushed with anger before he swore and grabbed the phone. His orders were terse, bitten out. He nodded once at the short reply. "She will be here in a few minutes."

Quin stared at him.

"Untouched," he admitted reluctantly.

"And?" The voice was even softer.

"She will stay that way. If you do your job before dawn comes to a new day."

Quin leaned against the door, knowing he had bought the only concessions he could. The difference of a few hours meant life or death. "I will wait."

Gustaf scowled angrily. "One day one of us from the old days will even a few scores," he promised furiously. He swore again when Quin showed no reaction. He had been so certain that he and his network had finally gotten a hold on the renegade gypsy. The job he had before him was only the tip of the assault planned. He wanted to throw this part into Quin's face until he and his woman choked on it. Instead he bided his time. Only the fact that the end for this enemy was so close on the horizon he could taste it kept him from using the gun that lay so silently in the drawer pressed against his belly.

The room was silent enough for the ticking of a clock to be heard. Quin watched the man who had had almost as many names as he. No matter how carefully he laid his new lives, there was always something that brought the hunters back. And with the hunters came the killing and the danger. Caprice now stood in the middle, an unarmed innocent in a war zone. He loved her but he had not been able to protect her from this. Guilt was an emotion he rarely felt, certainly not since he reached his maturity. But guilt rode him now like a scorned mistress. For her sake, he would sell his honor, what there was of it, to this killer who looked at him with eyes that laughed at others' pain. He would see her safe, but from that moment, Randall Quinlan would cease to exist for her. It was the only way to insure her life.

Caprice sat completely still as she swayed with the movement of the car. She was blindfolded, her hands tied behind her. Only her mouth and feet were free. Little good that did her. The man who had been described to her by the runner sat beside her, saying nothing. Silently cursing her stupidity, especially when Quin had warned her against leaving the building or even going downstairs until he came for her, she tried to still her anger enough to think. She didn't know where they were or even where they were going. The few sounds she could detect through the closed, black-tinted windows of the limousine hinted that they were still near people, not in the open country. Suddenly, the car made a sharp turn. Unprepared, she lurched against the bulk beside her.

The man hissed furiously, his fingers curling around her shoulder. His touch dug in for a second, then his hold changed slightly. "The gypsy chooses well, as always," he murmured in a thick accent.

Caprice froze. Every instinct screamed with the invasion of her personal space. Every sense rebelled at any other man's hands but Quin's on her body. But beneath all of that, fear spread like an insidious disease, robbing her of anger and logic for a few precious heartbeats. But despite the fear, she didn't plead. Silence was a weapon, too, and she used it.

"So you fight." The hand stroked her skin lightly, almost delicately. "Good. I like that." His fingers trailed down her arm, then slipped away. "I shall make certain there is time when this is over for us to become very close." He set her back in her place, laughing softly. "Very close, indeed."

Caprice leaned against the door, breathing slowly and deeply. Every woman's nightmare. But she would survive. Death left no hope of freedom. But life promised everything if one was just strong enough to seal off the pain. She had done it before. She would do it again, if she had to. Only this time she was not alone. Quin was out there somewhere. And she knew the man whom she called lover. He would not stop until he found her. And if this excuse for a human carried out his threat before Quin could find her, they would deal with that, too. With the knowledge of Quin and his code of honor, some of the fear left her. The anger came back, cold like his, silent and soul-deep. She had one assignment. Survive and wait for Quin to find her.

* * *

Quin heard voices in the outer hall. He moved away from the door, standing to one side so that whoever entered would not see him at first. He didn't look at Gustaf. Until the job was done, his physical safety was guaranteed from that direction. The door opened. Caprice was the first one through. Only training and the life he had led gave him the ability to look at the rope biting into her wrists, the paleness of her face around the tight blindfold, and the rough male grip on her arm without any visible reaction. Inside was a different matter. Every indignity was a score multiplied tenfold that he would settle for her. He looked her over briefly but thoroughly, then focused on Gustaf's angry face.

"I want five minutes."

Gustaf shook his head.

Quin shrugged and started for the door.

"No!" Gustaf surged to his feet, bracing his hands on the desk. "Damn you, I give the orders here."

"Then do it or I walk."

Gustaf measured his determination for a long minute, his chest heaving with the force of holding his temper. Finally, with an angry slash of his hand, he commanded the man holding on to Caprice to release her and leave. "I will stay."

Quin turned back to the door.

"There are other men."

Quin was a step deep into the hall when Gustaf swore an oath Quin hadn't heard since his youth.

"All right. Have your last moments with this woman." He stalked around the desk and into the hall, his glare murderous. "It will change nothing."

Quin smiled slightly, a grim twist of his lips that his tormentor recognized. The gypsy never smiled for real, except when he was making a promise that was fulfilled in hell. Despite himself, despite the plans that he and his associates had set up, plans that would remove the gypsy as though he had never been, Gustaf felt the whispery touch of fear. For one instant, it lay like a dark veil across his madness. Quin registered the change, accepted it, and played to it. He would use any advantage for Caprice's sake.

"If she is harmed, by anyone, for any reason, if there is one bruise on her skin, one whisper from her lips of any of your people so much as saying a curse in front of her, I will stalk you, take everything from you but the breath in your body. You will beg to do penance to her for the rest of whatever will be left of your life."

Gustaf stepped back a pace, staring at the man whose soft voice held not one hint of anger, only an indifference that was impossible to face. "I gave you my word," he rasped.

"And we both know just how good that is."

Gustaf swallowed heavily as Quin turned from him and entered the study, closing the door behind him.

Quin didn't waste time checking to see if Gustaf was listening or had stationed one of his men to do so. He walked across the room and released Caprice's blindfold, then turned her quickly, retying her bonds so that she was still imprisoned but without the visible damage that the other knots had been causing.

Caprice blinked, for those first few seconds having trouble adjusting to the sunlight pouring into the room. By the time she could see properly, Quin had turned her around to face him again.

"Did he touch you?"

One look at those eyes and Caprice changed the first answer she would have given. "No."

Quin searched her expression, seeing the first lie on her lips, in her eyes. For him, she risked it. "You're lying but it doesn't matter." He pulled her against him, needing to feel her heart beating strongly to the time of his. "Whatever they tell you to do, don't fight them. Just do it."

Caprice absorbed his strength and his warmth, her eyes closed. "All right."

He cupped her chin, raising her face to his. "They won't hurt you. You're a hostage to them. Not a danger as long as you don't see their faces. So I'll have to blindfold you again before they come back."

She nodded, trusting him with her life. "I understand."

He shook his head, his mouth a grim line. "No, you don't. And I'm not going to explain. But I am going to make you a promise. You won't ever have to face this again."

If her hands had been free, Caprice would have held him tight. "Don't put any more scars on your soul for me," she pleaded.

Rejection of her words was in every taut line of his body. "I don't have a soul."

"Yes, you do. I found it and I'm not letting it or you go."

Quin didn't allow himself to react to her declaration. He knew what had to be done. Even she could not turn him now. A thump at the door signaled their time was up. Quin picked up the blindfold from the desk.

Caprice read the hell in his eyes, a hell that he would not or, perhaps, could not release. Her arms ached to hold him. "I remember when you told me to close my eyes that night," she whispered softly. If she could not save him from hell, then, at least she could give him a memory to stop even a second of the pain. "Darkness is for secrets. I won't be thinking of them in my darkness. It will be your face, your memory I will hold."

Quin stared into her eyes as he raised the cloth to cover them. Speech was impossible. The future, ashes of his lost honor. Caprice, his dream breathing and loving. He tied the final knot, then bent his head to brush her lips. He had offered her passion, love, danger, and lies. He had never offered her tenderness until now.

"Dream for me, warrior maid, until I come for you." Her smile was the scar on his soul, cutting deeper than all the others. He turned from it, the present and future written in the red stains of the past.

Twelve

"You can't do it," Killian said harshly at the end of Quin's brief summation of the situation, Caprice's hostage status, and the price for her freedom.

Quin stripped out of his slacks and shirt, ignoring Killian's anger. His mind was racing time and death to find impossible answers for the woman he loved. Killian's emotions had no place in his thoughts. "That was the deal. I'm buying her out of there."

Killian rammed his hands in his pockets, fighting his anger for sanity. "You're signing your own death warrant. And you have never been an assassin in your life. I won't believe you would become one now."

Quin didn't try to refute the argument. There just wasn't time. He was making the wildest gamble of his life.

Killian stared at the mesh of scars on Quin's broad back. He had seen them too many times before to really react to the sight, terrible though it was. He frowned, thinking quickly, knowing that time was running out like water pouring out of a sieve. "It can't be this simple."

Quin yanked on a pair of black cotton pants and a shirt to match. "Her life. Did you honestly think I would play games with it?"

"I know you wouldn't." Killian caught his shoulder, dragging Quin around to face him. "Talk to me, damn you. I'll help with whatever plan you have in mind. I owe you. And I'm as rabid about paying debts as you are. And Caprice is my sister-in-law."

With another man, Quin might have had a hope of winning a battle of wills. But he knew Killian. The shorter man was the only person apart from Caprice he really trusted completely and the only one who might just be able to give him the edge he needed to take this last risk. "It isn't legal."

"I don't give a damn," Killian scowled. "And don't bother telling me I'm laying my life on the line either. I know the game and the rules. I may be out of the business, but I remember too well how it's played."

"I know where the target is. Not here, but close. I'm flying in tonight. I'll do the job and fly out."

"Pull the other one. The target you mentioned earlier is not someone you would take down. What's the rest of the plan?" he demanded flatly.

Quin sighed deeply. "Take the plan as stated, Kill."

The unthinkable was digging into his mind as he stared at Quin's implacable expression. "No."

Quin looked at him, furious, too aware of the minutes of Caprice's captivity sweeping by. "It's all you're getting."

"No, it isn't. You tell me what you are really planning. I know you, as much as you'll allow anyway. You aren't killing a man this way. Like I said, you've never been an assassin even if the target deserved a whole clip emptied into his brain. And this one doesn't."

"The price is Caprice."

"I know that," Killian snapped. "And you're wasting time trying to snow-job me."

Quin headed for the sitting room of the suite. "All right. You want the whole thing." He picked up a folder and thrust it at Killian. "That's what is going on. Why I'm being drawn into this spider's web. The trap within a trap, the plan within a plan. And I shall allow it to occur. But first I shall buy Caprice's life. One more sin won't matter."

Killian scanned the information that outlined a complex set of circumstances not only to unearth Quin's talent, utilizing it for a tricky if not impossible assassination plot, but also to draw him out of his lair long enough to activate a set of spies to follow him to ground when he retreated from the furor of his completed assignment. From there an assault would be launched to wipe him from the face of existence. Killian raised his eyes, focusing on Quin's grim expression.

"What about Caprice?"

"You're going to get her out of there while I do a little shooting." He picked up another envelope, this one smaller, and passed it to him. "That is a complete layout of the estate where Gustaf is holding her, the security system and guard schedules." He nodded toward a big backpack sitting beside the door. "That's for you. Inside, you'll find a dart gun and drugs for the sentries and dogs. An untraceable gun, two knives, and a few smoke bombs. Gato, Sandor, and Ivan, equally equipped, are waiting downstairs to take you to the estate and to guard your back while you get Caprice out. At exactly three this morning, there will be a rather noisy diversion next door. Lots of fire, extra people, confusion. That will be your cover to go over the south wall. The only thing I don't have is Caprice's exact location."

"You moved fast," Killian muttered.

Quin shrugged. If it hadn't been for the flight time of pulling his staff from the island, he would have moved faster. "Time matters."

"How are you going to fake the takedown?"

Quin turned from him. "I am not."

Killian stared at the man he would have sworn he knew. "Turn around," he commanded. "And tell me that."

Quin faced him. "I am not going to fake it. It's too easy for that to be disproved. Gustaf will probably send a man to confirm the hit. How the hell do you think I'm going to be able to fake it in this short time?"

"You can try."

"Would you if it were Silke?"

Both men, neither strangers to risks involving life and death, faced their truths. Killian sighed deeply, angrily. "I can't sit by and let you do this, no matter what I might feel personally."

"You won't be sitting by. Why do you think I have three men downstairs? Force me to it and they can be your jailers until it is too late for you to do anything but rescue Caprice." Quin slipped on his shoulder holster, checked the clip in his handmade gun, and slid the weapon into the sheath. "I shall not take chances with her life, even for you."

"And if I refuse to go on with the plan to get her out?"

"You have never been able to bluff me." Quin smiled gently, his eyes silver ice with no quarter offered or given. "My people are well trained. I would rather you were there for Caprice, a familiar face, but I will go with the talent I must."

Killian's curse was one that Quin had taught him. There was no going back for any of them. "For her sake and Silke's, I'll be there. Beyond that, there will be nothing left."

Quin inclined his head, expecting no less. As Killian had gotten a measure of his honor over the years of their association, he, too, had gleaned the same depth. That had made the course he had chosen the only available option. The die had been cast too long ago to be changed now.

Killian stared at the house to which Quin had directed him. Quin's men were spread out behind him. He heard no sound, but he was aware of their support. In the distance he could hear nothing but the creatures of the night as they went about their hunting. The cloak of darkness was too familiar, the need for accuracy no less so. Angling his head as he heard the prearranged diversion begin, he signaled silently for the plan to begin. Gato would take out the dogs. Ivan, the guards, while the last of the trio would take care of the security system. Once they were inside, Gato and Sandor would stand guards. Ivan would do the point sweep until they'd found Caprice. Moving soundlessly, each of them became a shadow to blend with the others. Killian didn't think about what Quin was doing or his own culpability. Quin had made certain that he would have no time or opportunity to contact the authorities anyway. He had one part to play and that was getting Caprice free.

Caprice cursed softly as she rubbed her face repeatedly against one of the carved posts of the four-poster bed. She was tired of being blind. She didn't know what Quin was doing, but she was positive he was coming for her. And she intended to be free to help, not trussed up like a sacrifice waiting to be barbecued. A second later, the cloth stealing her sight fell away. She blinked in the darkness, not having expected it.

"Oh well," she muttered, turning her attention to the next piece of business. She dropped down on the mattress on her back and tried to slip her lower body through the loop of her secured arms. "Damn," she panted a few futile minutes later.

Her wrists burned like fire and she still hadn't succeeded. Rising awkwardly, she bumped her way around the room, making as little noise as possible. Finally, she found the bathroom. But it was clean of anything she could use for a knife. Just as she was about to turn away, she caught the glitter of the mirror lying on the vanity. It was one of the handheld kind. Turning her back to it, she picked it up, felt its weight, closed her eyes in a swift prayer, and smashed it against the edge of the tub. Being careful not to step on the pieces, she closed the bathroom door so that she could risk the light. Only two fragments were big enough to work with, but they were enough. Sitting down on the floor, she fumbled through the shards for the first. The minutes dripped by as she worked. More than once she inhaled sharply as her need to free herself caused her hands to slip and her skin to bear the marks of her mistakes. She could feel the warm stickiness of her own blood but she worked on. Quin was coming and she would be ready.

"You first," Quin commanded, urging the chief of security in front of him as they crossed the last feet to the back door of the main house.

The man said nothing but obeyed the prod reluctantly. He led the way up through the darkened interior to the upstairs master suite. The room was dark, the shape on the bed nothing more than a lump in the gloom. The moment the door was shut behind them, Quin tapped his prisoner lightly at the back of his neck, effectively removing any threat he might have been as he fell to the floor unconscious. Then Quin eased toward the window, drawing back the drapes as per last-minute instructions from Gustaf to give the man who had been sent to watch him work a clear field of vision. With the night glasses he undoubtedly had, he would miss none of the action. Quin turned, taking aim and fired at the bed. The shot was nothing more than a faint snap of sound. The lump didn't move. Quin nodded once, closed the drapes, and left the way that he had come.

Killian gestured toward the final door at the end of the long hall of bedrooms. Caprice had to be there. He opened it, finding the ink of total darkness. His backup stayed in the hall to ensure he would have warning if they were discovered. "Caprice," he called softly, seeing the faint rim of light under the closed door on his right.

Caprice flinched at the sound of her name just as the last bond dropped free. Scrambling to her feet, she hardly noticed her bleeding wrists as she flipped off the light. Waiting in the darkness, she listened for any sound to identify the voice. One thing she knew. It wasn't Quin.

Killian moved closer to the door but didn't try to open it. If Caprice was in the building, she had to be behind it. But if they had gotten her away, he might just get himself killed and that ultimately translated into no chance for Caprice. "Do you remember the night you and a vodka bottle had fun at Silke's apartment?" he asked, softly, using the only thing that came to mind that would identify himself to her if his voice did not.

Caprice froze. Only Silke could have told anyone about that, and the only person she might have told would be Killian. "Killian?" she hissed.

"In the flesh, honey. I'm here to take you home."

Caprice eased open the door. His hand was there to take hers. He swore roughly on feeling the blood.

"What did they do to you?" he demanded, his fingers tracing the wounds on her skin.

"They didn't do anything. I did it getting untied. Don't worry about it. I'll survive." She tried to shake off his hold but couldn't. "Where's Quin? Did you split up to look for me?"

Killian urged her toward the door. "He's around," he murmured in a deliberately vague tone he hoped she would accept without any more questions.

"Is he all right?" Caprice returned sharply, something in his voice alerting her to a problem.

"Quin is always all right. Now, shut up so we will be too. I want to get out of here in one piece."

He waited for a second to be certain she understood, then he opened the door, checking the corridor and his backup before he allowed her into the lighted hall. Caprice followed Killian, but with every step the conviction that something was terribly wrong settled more heavily about her. By the time they reached the car and Quin still hadn't joined them, she stopped.

"Where is Quin? I'm not leaving here until I'm sure he's all right."

Killian assessed her stance and her expression. She was more angry than afraid. Maybe he could risk telling her. "He isn't here. The price of your freedom was a job. He's doing it. He's not even in the city."

Caprice absorbed the information, her belief in the man she loved still not shaken. She didn't understand why he hadn't come after her himself and skipped the assignment. "What aren't you telling me?"

"Not here." Killian took her arm in an unbreakable grip and urged her into the car. "I'll explain everything I know when we get out of here."

"Bull's eye."

Gustaf smiled in satisfaction as he pressed the phone more tightly to his ear. "You are certain?" he demanded of his man. "You saw the hit?"

"The gypsy opened the drapes. I saw him do the hit, and then leave."

Gustaf's smile died. "He did not kill the security chief?"

"I don't know. Is it important?"

Frowning, Gustaf considered that. "I do not know. Do not lose our friend on his way back here. I would not like to know you failed."

"I won't lose him," he promised before he hung up.

"Why are we going to the airport?" Caprice demanded, glaring at Killian's face as he worked on her wrists. She didn't feel the sting of the antiseptic that he was using. She only had one thought on her mind. Quin. "Is Quin waiting there?"

"I don't know. It doesn't matter anyway." Caprice jerked her hands away. "What do you mean, it doesn't matter? It matters to me. What aren't you telling me? Is he dead? Is that it?" Even saying the word, cut more deeply than any knife. She would know if he were dead. She would feel it to her soul.

Killian looked up, judging her mood, furious that Quin had reached her so deeply. He sighed, feeling more tired than he could ever remember. He didn't want to be the man to tell her what must be said. He didn't want to see what his words would mean to her. And more importantly, he didn't want to have to force her to leave the city with him as he suspected he would have to do when she learned the truth.

"Tell me," Caprice commanded, looking him straight in the eye.

Killian inclined his head, settled back on his side of the limo, and watched her expression as he slowly and carefully gave her every fact he knew. He saw her pale, her hands clenching in rejection, the bandages around her wrists only a few shades lighter than her flesh.

"It isn't true," she breathed angrily. "He told me he wasn't an assassin. I know he didn't lie."

"His whole life is a lie."

"I know about his name changes, his past. He told me that too," she dismissed impatiently. "I don't give a damn. I love him. You ought to know what it feels like, or are you lying to my sister?"

Killian's jaw tightened as he fought not to retaliate. "You know I'm not."

"And I know Quin. He wouldn't do what you're saying. He has a plan."

"There wasn't time for a plan. This isn't the damn movies. Gustaf only gave his word to keep you unharmed for this night. He would have started working on you, probably in the morning. That's the kind of man he is. Quin knew that," he said roughly, knowing subtlety and gentleness wouldn't get this job done. "I wouldn't have gone along with this assassination if he hadn't literally kept me under guard until he handed me over to his men. By then it was too late to do anything even if I had been willing to let you die to save the target."

Caprice inhaled sharply, the thrust going home. Quin had sold his honor for her life. And he had sold one life in her place. One more scar for his soul because of her. Tears she hadn't shed for herself filled her eyes. "Another scar on his soul," she whispered, not even thinking of the one on her own.

Killian wanted to touch her then, wanted to hold her as she needed to be held. But every line of her body screamed a silent rejection. She wanted no other arms but Quin's.

"There's more, isn't there?" she demanded of him. Her world was shattering in a million pieces and still she sensed that more pain was to come.

"We're leaving the city." Before she could protest, he raised his hand to silence her. "Quin doesn't want you here any longer. And even if you stay, it will make no difference. He won't be here. He's going back to the island."

Caprice stared at him, hearing the certainty in his voice as though it came from a long distance away. The pity in his eyes almost broke her for a second. "No. I won't believe it until he tells me himself. You'll have to tie me back up, gag me, knock me unconscious, but I'm not going until he tells me himself that I must."

Surprised at her determination even in the face of all he had told her, Killian tried to reason with her. "You aren't thinking clearly. You know what he's done for you. I won't believe you can live with that."

"I don't know anymore what I can do. I hurt, Killian. But I love him. I still don't believe he would do as you say. There must be some other explanation." By the time she finished she was almost pleading with him to tell her his words were lies.

Steeling himself against her need, Killian touched a button at his side to open a small compartment. He took out the slim gray case inside and lifted the lid to show her the tiny vial and hypodermic inside. "He sent these for you. My last resort so that you wouldn't be hurt." He watched her face change, hating himself and Quin in that moment with almost equal intensity.

Caprice stared at the setup, too stunned to speak. She had been so certain she knew Quin. The man she loved would not have done this. Hope faltered, battered not by her experiences but by his seeming betrayal of all they had shared.

"Don't make me use them. I'll hate it, but I'll do it. I won't take you home in a box to the woman I love and to the family I respect. I won't see your eyes closed forever because I felt the agony of what you're feeling."

Caprice stared at the needle, one final question pushing through the pain. She raised her head. "Does he believe in your ability so much that he made no plans to check if I got free?"

Killian hesitated.

Caprice read the pause. "He will be at the airport."

"Maybe," he allowed cautiously.

She leaned back in the seat, turning her head to look out the window. "You won't need the drug. I won't fight."

Quin shifted in the seat as the plane lifted off the ground. He was taking a risk in going back to Houston, but he had to see for himself that Caprice was safe. It would be his last memory of her in the future he had written for himself. Rolling his shoulders, he eased the tension from his body. In a few hours, if he was lucky, Gustaf would discover his little plan had failed. His fury at losing not only the hit but the leverage would have no equal. He would come hunting. Quin smiled grimly. The plan within a plan was coming to fruition nicely. Reaching for the phone; he implemented the next phase. His staff, including the men who had helped Killian, would soon be on the way home, a list of instructions in hand. As the jet screamed across the night sky, he laid his future out brick by brick, each call, each debt collected providing one more stone.

Thirteen

Caprice stared out the window of the limo, watching without really seeing as the big car slipped into the private plane area of the terminal. Nothing made sense. Killian just expected her to walk away from Quin without a fight. Quin expected it. How could either of them believe that of her? Maybe Killian could be forgiven. He didn't know her that well, but Quin did. Quin understood. They had spoken words to each other, words stronger than those whispered in the heat of passion. Neither of them loved easily, but they had made a commitment. She could not believe that Quin had gone back on that. She could not believe that he would walk away and never come back. So many questions and no answers. Her chin lifted. She would not leave without those answers. She turned her head just as the car pulled to a stop. If her future was ashes, she, at least, would see the last of the fire burned out.

"I'm not going. You might as well get the drug out." She looked Killian straight in the eye.

Killian stared back at her, his gaze measuring her determination. Silke had that kind of look when nothing was going to budge her. "I've done worse things," he murmured, testing her.

"Probably. I don't care. You must have a way of contacting him. Even if all you say is true, he would have wanted either a verbal or visual confirmation that you got me out."

Killian's brows rose at the deduction. "I didn't expect you to know him that well."

"Neither of you seems to have expected anything of me but to be some obedient female so grateful for her life that she would run home with her tail between her legs." Her hands clenched into fists at her sides. "Well, I'm not. I want to see him. Failing that, talking will do. Arrange it."

"Giving orders."

She nodded once, sharply, then folded her arms across her middle and waited.

While Caprice had been doing her thinking, Killian had been doing some of his own. Quin had left him with cleanup detail. He would have handled that, but something about Caprice bothered him. She wasn't behaving as Quin had led him to believe. There was a depth of commitment about her that suggested a lot more than just being Quin's lover. And despite this mess tonight, Killian did know Quin. It was completely out of character for him to have allowed this to happen without trying to stop it. Plus, there was the prophecy. He knew why Quin had come to Houston. He doubted Caprice did.

"All right," he said at last.

Caprice searched his face, checking for some trick or evasion. She found nothing but a steadiness that said he would back her.

"He is here. His plane should have landed by now. But it is only a stop to make sure you are safe."

"How were you going to report?"

"I still am." He silenced her protest with a gesture. "I'll go over and talk to him, tell him what you told me. The decision is his. That's as far as I'm prepared to go. After that it's either a battle or you accept he doesn't want to see you."

"We'll see," she murmured stubbornly.

Killian scowled. "I mean it."

"So do I," she snapped back.

Killian swore and got out of the car. Before he slammed the door, he demanded, "I want your word you'll stay here until I get back. You're still not out of danger."

"I'll stay but that is the last promise I'm giving you."

Quin studied Killian as he entered the plane, relaxing when he scanned his expression. Although Gato had notified him by phone that they had gotten Caprice away safely, Quin needed more. "How is she?"

Killian dropped into the executive chair across from the desk. "Mad as hell. Stubborn as a mule and smart enough to have your number. She's not budging without using that damn drug until you talk to her. She doesn't believe you're sending her away for good. Just what the devil has been going on between the two of you? You know who she is. And I know what she meant to you when you left Atlanta. In spite of the relative safety you've had these last couple of years, you risked something staying out in the open all these weeks just to be with her. And there is that damn prophecy."

Quin didn't betray his unease with even a flicker of an eyelash. Too much rode on his decisions, Caprice's life the most important of all the stakes. "You know she has to get on that plane."

"Then you put her there. I damn well am not doing your dirty work. You took her to bed. You made her believe in you in the face of odds that would have brought a lesser woman to her knees. I'm not going back over to that car and strong-arm her, jab a needle in her vein, and carry her like a sack of potatoes out of here. She deserves better than that."

"She deserves to live," Quin shot back, his temper flaring as it never had before.

Killian's brows rose, reading something dark and hurting in Quin's eyes. Stunned, he sat back. "My God. You're as bad as she is. The prophecy is true."

Silently cursing himself, Quin grabbed hold of his temper and his control. There would be no more betrayals. "It's true. But Randall Quinlan is no longer safe enough for any kind of life. I fooled myself once and damn near got her killed. I won't ever face what happened tonight. And I certainly won't ever ask Caprice to relive this horror in another place or time."

Killian knew he would have felt the same if Silke were the woman and he the man in the same situation. "Then tell her that. Maybe she'll believe you. She won't believe me. Even when I told her you killed a man to save her life, she didn't believe it," he added harshly, his own part in that segment of the plan still eating at him.

For the first time in his life, Quin wondered if he would have the strength to do what must be done to free Caprice. He had known he could rescue her from Gustaf; the only uncertainty had been limiting the amount of trauma to Caprice. But this was different. He would have to look her in the eye and tell her that he did not want her anymore. He sighed deeply and pushed to his feet.

"Let's go."

Neither man spoke as they covered the distance between planes. Everything that could be said had been.

"I'll wait here," Killian murmured quietly, stopping beside the steps leading to the aircraft that would take them home. He gestured to the driver, who was one of his own men, to leave the car.

Quin nodded but didn't hesitate in his stride to cross the last feet to Caprice. He opened the car door, vaguely surprised she hadn't gotten out to meet him. When he slipped inside and got his first look at her eyes, he knew why.

Caprice stared at him, searching for any sign of injury. Relief diluted her anger for a second when she found no new scars. Then she focused on his face and the clear purpose she read in his eyes. The anger came back, stronger than ever. "Now tell me those lies you told Killian," she challenged.

Quin studied her silently for a moment. The situation was even worse than he could have foreseen. No wonder Killian was furious. "They weren't lies. I am sending you away," he stated finally, his eyes unreadable in the light that Caprice had turned on.

"For how long, Quin? How long are you exiling me?"

"It's not exile. It's removal." He watched her pale. Looking away from the pain she tried to hide and couldn't, he noticed the strips of white around her wrists. His features tautened as he reached out, catching her forearms and drawing her limbs out to their full length. "How did you get these?" He demanded softly, his voice too gentle to be anything but the eye of fury before an explosion.

Caprice stared down at the bandages, not seeing the gauze, only remembering the way she had hung on to her belief in the man who had promised her love and offered her exile forever. She hurt. She had been so sure that Killian was wrong. "Let me go," she whispered, suddenly too tired to fight anymore.

"Tell me what happened. Who did this to you?" Quin ordered, not hearing the weariness that stole the anger from her tone. He rotated her wrists, seeing the thin streaks of blood that marked each slash beneath the covering of cloth. "Gustaf gave me his word that you would be safe tonight. What did he do?" The scars that Gustaf had put on his body hadn't hurt nearly as much. He looked up, focusing on the sick look in Caprice's eyes. Every nerve tightened, shutting down at the agony in her expression. "Tell me," he commanded in that same gentle tone that always whispered before the gypsy appeared from behind the disguise of Quin.

Caprice shivered as she stared into his eyes. The past was alive as it had never been. Gustaf had been unable to show her this. Killian had been unable to tell her and make her believe it. Yet Quin's soft, almost genial tone convinced her. "No one did anything to me. I did it myself."

"How?" He stroked her wrists lightly, just above the gauze. "I retied the ropes. They wouldn't have done any damage even if you had struggled."

"I didn't sit around waiting for rescue. I cut myself loose." Even though his touch carried no pressure, Caprice knew better than to try to pull away. But she wanted to. She hurt too much to want his hands on her, reminding her of the empty darkness and the cold that hovered only seconds away, enemies from which there would be no escape when Quin sent her away.

"With what?"

"A mirror. I broke it and I used the shards as knives. I just wasn't as neat as I would have liked."

Quin closed his eyes against the truth. He knew how glass could cut, knew the pain of each miss, the desperation that would have forced her to continue in spite of the fire burning into her with each mistake. He had been wrong about her. He had thought he had known her, her reactions, her needs, her hopes for that future that was so very important to her. But in all those facts, nothing had prepared him for seeing what she had risked, the pain and the reprisals that would have come if Gustaf had discovered what she had done.

"I told you to wait," he said at last.

"In our darkness."

At her reply, his eyes opened. Memories were all that he would have in the future. Even these memories were better than her absence.

"You also said to think of what we had done in the darkness." This time it was her voice that flowed effortlessly and gently with each word. she was learning, learning from Quin to walk in the world that named him both hunter and hunted. "I relived every second, tasted again your flesh, inhaled our scent at the moment of completion, union of two to one. Although neither of us ever said the word, I heard love on your lips. On mine." She smiled, the curve of her lips unknowingly a match to his own when he was setting a trap. "Truth. Ours." She felt his fingers release her, Quin sliding away from her, from the weapons that she made of her words. Without looking down, she turned her hands so that now she held him, his heat sharing life with hers, a mating that was, in a way, as intimate as their lovemaking. "Only it wasn't a truth at all. Those words were obscene lies to trick, to delude, to steal from me what I would have freely given without the lies."

If he had not heard the agony, if he had not seen the smile,

Quin might have been able to free himself, slip from the car into the night, and walk away. But he did see, too much. In that second he learned that many scars were more lethal and damaging than their more showy physical counterparts. "It was no lie. I did love you then. I love you now." If the word would help her leave, he would use it.

The smile deepened, the fury smoldering in eyes that had once burned only with the fire of desire. "If that is supposed to make me feel better, it falls short of the mark." She released him, leaning away as far as the cushions behind her would permit. She no longer wanted his warmth any more than she wanted his lies. "Go. You said you were leaving. Do it."

Quin bent to her, his hands capturing her shoulders before she realized what he intended. "No. You started this. You would not accept what I was doing. I wanted to spare us both this. I thought I could free you without having to hurt either of us with the truth. I was wrong.

"I've heard your truth." She nodded toward the compartment that held the vial. "I saw your methods. A man I thought I could trust is ready to use that on me at your command."

Quin ignored the reference to Killian. "When Gustaf took you this afternoon, I was on a one-way trip into hell and so were you. He would have killed you, and it wouldn't have been fast or easy. It would have been slow, and every inch would have been a journey into a nightmare you can't even begin to imagine. I've been down that road and survived."

Caprice stared into his face, remembering the scars on his body. Suddenly the past had a definition she hadn't expected. "He put them there?" she whispered, this time her voice the voice of a woman hurting for her man.

He nodded shortly, not really caring any longer about Gustaf's brand on his flesh. If it helped Caprice to see, every second he had lived then and since was worth the price. "He offered me this night of guaranteed safety for you. He didn't think I would be able to outfox him with so little time."

Even though he knew the stakes, Quin's decision hurt her. Because of the danger in which she had stood, Quin had taken a man's life. "Killian told me what you did."

Quin paused. He could allow her to believe the lie he had told

Killian. He had thought it would make it easier for her. Maybe he had been wrong. "What he thinks I did."

Caprice wrapped her hands around his wrists, no longer needing to be free. Hope breathed a warming fire in her heart. She held his eyes, praying as she hadn't needed to do in the middle of the worst of her captivity. "You didn't do it?"

Quin read the hope she was making no effort to disguise. Torture would have been easier to withstand. "No. I set the scene to make it look as if I did."

"How?"

He shook his head, wiping away with one gesture the hurried and desperate chances he had taken to free her. "It doesn't matter except in its effect on you. That is one of the reasons you have to get out of the city quickly. Gustaf won't be fooled forever. Even now the man he sent to confirm the hit could have discovered the truth."

Caprice hardly noticed the renewed danger in which she stood. Her concern was centered on Quin, on what his choices could mean to his safety. "Gustaf will come looking for you, perhaps follow you to the island."

He inclined his head, trying to block out the fierce light of loyalty and love that shone bright as a midday sun in her eyes. "He will find me. I won't be hiding."

Caprice stared at him, unable to believe that he would just sit and wait. "But you have defenses there," she said, trying to understand the nuances she could hear in Quin's voice. Defeat? An unthinkable possibility. Resignation? The reaction didn't fit the man she had come to love.

"There is no such thing as an impregnable hideaway."

She fought the realization that for whatever reason Quin wanted Gustaf to find him. He intended a confrontation. The memory of the man who had held her life in his hands, the man who had scarred Quin so terribly, chilled her. "Then die again," she whispered.

Quin sighed deeply, letting the weariness that lived in his soul surface. "Even a cat has a limited number of lives. I survive. But some days it is not truly worth the price. This is why you will not come with me. I would have sold my soul, my honor, and my body for you this night. I could have lived with that to have you.

But could you? Sometime, maybe one day when we were the happiest, you would remember what I would have done tonight if all else had failed, maybe even other nights, to keep you safe. How would you feel? Guilty. Hating the price you had to pay to share my shadows, looking around each corner, waiting for some unknown enemy from my past to use you to buy yet another piece of me. How many times will I see you bound, held as a hostage? That could be our future. In many ways it is more real than our love. Could you live that and survive as the woman you are? If I can be broken, it will be by you, the prices you have to pay to stay with me. If I truly loved you, would I ask this of you? Would you ask it of me?"

Caprice stared at him, reading the future as he painted it, a future that would burn them alive. She had seen only the love, the fire he created in the darkness that was their own because they had made it so. Quin was stronger than she. He saw reality beyond the emotion. He saw what could not be changed simply because they loved. As the truth seeped in, so did the cold, soul-deep and heart-wide. This darkness was an alien world that would carry her footprints into eternity.

"It isn't that I don't love you enough. It is that I love you, too much." He drew her toward him, across the space between the seats and into his lap. He cradled her close, inhaling her scent, committing it to memory for there would never be another woman like her for him. His hands molded her form, one last tactile memory that would come alive with every new breath. "I would rather you lived, shared your passion with another man, gave another promises that you would have given me than to tear you apart with any of those moments of darkness."

Caprice laid her hand on his heart, feeling the strong, sure beat to match her own. There were no words to erase the truth, to breathe life into hope and a belief in the future that would never be. Moving her hand, she leaned her head against his chest and closed her eyes. "Then hold me. Just for a little while. Make the darkness ours one more time."

Quin wrapped his arms around her, absorbing her acceptance, his eyes as bleak as her voice. Seconds of time had wings. The night sped past to end in a soft rap against the window of the car. Quin cupped her chin, bringing her face up. Her lashes were silvery feathers on her cheeks. They fluttered, started to open. "Don't. Remember the darkness that was once ours. Kiss me from there, and let me leave you from there. In that place there was always hope, always a tomorrow to be found and shared."

Tears stung Caprice's eyes at the words of the poet who made love with such beauty. He had filled the darkness with pleasure without end. True hope in their world that no longer had any. "Kiss me once, then go, my love."

Quin bent his head, taking her lips, not in passion. There was no room for something so transient. Instead he gave his soul. Where he was going he would not need it.

Caprice held herself still as Quin raised his head. His taste was on her lips, his scent a blanket of fragrance that would fade in a moment. Even his warmth left her as he gently slipped her onto the seat beside him, his hands lingering briefly on the bundle of nerves that no man would ever know enough to touch. The pleasure came even as the car door opened and the night-colored past that would always haunt him stole him from her.

Fourteen

Caprice stared into the night, ignoring Killian as he watched her from his seat on the other side of the corporate jet. She knew he was worried. At another time she would have, at least, made an attempt to set his mind at rest. But there was no rest, not for either of them. The future was a bleak tapestry of broken dreams. She lived. Quin lived. That was the most she could ask. As he had said, better that than things that could never be. Wrapping her arms around her stomach, she swallowed carefully. The physical impact of the kidnapping and Quin's leaving had arrived almost at the moment the plane had lifted into the sky. If she had eaten at any time in the last few hours, she would have been worrying if she would be able to avoid disgracing herself.

"Are you sure I can't get you something to drink?" Killian asked quietly.

Caprice turned her head, her gaze registering his concern but her mind refusing to be touched by it. There was room in her thoughts, her emotions, her life, for no one but Quin. "No, I'm fine."

"You don't look it," he stated bluntly.

She shrugged, turning back to the night. "You wouldn't either if you had just seen Silke for the last time."

Killian inhaled in a sharp hiss. That one sentence was enough. He said no more.

Caprice fought the steadily worsening nausea for the rest of the flight home. By the time they landed, she was barely able to swallow without feeling as though she wouldn't last another minute.

"You're coming home with me. You don't look like you're up to the drive to your parents' house," Killian muttered, taking her arm as they started to leave the plane.

"No." Caprice gulped hurriedly, wishing she were anywhere quiet and private.

"Yes. So help me I'll throw you over my shoulder if I have to."

"Then you'll clean up a mess," she warned as he stuffed her into the limo waiting for them at the gate.

He glared at her as he climbed in after her. "Where you and Quin are concerned, that seems to be my role in life." Before she could rebut this, he spoke to the driver, giving him the new directions. "And before you say anything, I'll take care of explaining to Lorraine and Geoffrey. Under the circumstances, they'll understand."

Caprice leaned back against the cushions. She just didn't have the strength to oppose Killian, not tonight. Tomorrow she would make arrangements of her own. Tonight she would accept a bed at Silke's.

"What do you mean he's not coming back for her?" Silke demanded, staring at her husband as he came out of their en suite bathroom in his robe. The night had been one long nightmare. Dawn had already come before the plane had touched down. She hadn't been at the airport. Killian had asked her to stay home. She had waited, a fresh pot of coffee ready, not that either Caprice or Killian had tried any. Caprice had looked ready to drop and wanted only a bed. Silke hadn't asked questions, just led the way. Killian had been in the shower when she had returned.

"I thought he loved her."

"He does." Killian sat down beside her on the bed and drew her close. He needed her in ways he hadn't expected. Caprice's comment had hit home. Silke was his life now. He didn't want to consider a world that they couldn't share. "But love doesn't always conquer all. Reality can be stronger. And in this case, it is. If he could have stayed, he would have. You didn't see his face when she was taken. I did. You don't know what he was prepared to do to free her. I do." Even now, he still remembered his relief when Quin had told him the truth about the hit. He sighed deeply. "And you don't know what death looks like walking away from you in the darkness, but I learned tonight. He's dying without her. But he would rather face that than having her in danger. And that won't change just because he loves her or she him. If anything, it makes the equation worse. He knew that and accepted it. If you care about Caprice, you'll have to accept it as well."

Silke's golden eyes glittered with frustration. "I can't look at her. She's suffering."

He stroked the hair back from her brow. "I know. And there isn't a thing we can do to help her. Only be there." He drew her against his chest.

Silke leaned into his strength, absorbing it with his words. She owed Caprice, but this was one debt she wouldn't be able to pay. No one could help Caprice but Quin, and he was gone.

Caprice stared at the shadows cast by the sun filtering through the drapes. She could hear the sounds of Killian leaving for the office and Silke moving carefully around the apartment. She should have been able to sleep from exhaustion if nothing else. But she hadn't closed her eyes yet. Her mind was a morass of memories. Her body was fighting a losing battle with nausea, and she was just too tired to care anymore. Rolling, over, she felt her stomach lurch one too many times. Half sliding out of the bed, she made it to the bathroom just in time to be very definitely sick. When it was over, she was almost reeling from the strain. But Silke was there, holding her head, saying nothing, asking no questions, simply being there. For three days, the bug continued to plague her and Silke was there, fielding concerned calls from her parents and sharing the night when sleep wouldn't come.

"You can't go on like this," Silke said quietly as she placed a mug of tea in front of Caprice and took the chair across from her. She studied Caprice's pale face, the circles under her eyes, the too thin lines of her body beneath the pullover and jeans she wore.

Caprice sipped at the tea, not really caring if she had the drink. She had agreed more to please Silke than from any real desire. "I made an appointment with the doctor for this afternoon. Maybe she can help," she murmured dully. Nothing seemed to matter now. She had called the doctor only because Silke had been threatening to do it herself. She knew it was time for her to pick up the pieces of her life and to get out of Silke's, but she just couldn't summon the energy or the drive to do anything. And that more than anything else but losing Quin frightened her. She was not a woman who rolled over in the face of adversity. Yet she couldn't shake the apathy or the illness dogging her footsteps.

"Well, at least that's a step in the right direction," Silke said after a moment. "What time do we leave?"

"You don't have to . . ."

Silke interrupted before she could finish. "I'm driving you. In the state you're in, you'd wreck the car." Silke got to her feet, glaring down at Caprice.

Caprice looked up at her, taking in the militant stance. She sighed and tried to pull herself together. "All right. You can drive me there, but I want you to drop me at my apartment when I'm done."

Silke shook her head. "We've been over this."

Caprice stood up slowly, carefully, forcing her mind and her body to take some definitive action. She couldn't keep sitting out her life. "I've stayed here long enough. You're hardly past your honeymoon. And I need to be alone now."

Silke could have fought the first part but not the second. She looked into Caprice's eyes and read the desperate emptiness that lived there. "We don't mind. And I would worry."

Caprice hesitated briefly, seeing Silke's needs as she wouldn't have been able to do in the past. "I love you," she murmured, for the first time saying the words aloud. She watched Silke's face change. Quin had left her a number of gifts even if he had left her a soul-deep emptiness. One was being able to express her emotions, her need for other people. "But I'm not staying."

Silke searched her expression, seeing the changes of the last weeks. Caprice had always been strong, but never gentle or intuitive. Suddenly, Silke could see those things lurking in the shadows of what Caprice had lost. "You'll call me if you need me?"

Caprice found a smile. It was small, hardly big enough to be noticed, but the effect was magnified by the very effort that went into its making. "Yes."

Silke exhaled deeply, finally feeling a small easing of the worry that had haunted her since she had opened the door to Caprice and gotten her first look at her sister's private hell. "I'll hold you to that," she said, as she picked up the mugs and carried them to the sink.

"Don't worry. I won't forget I said it," Caprice replied quietly.

"You're pregnant."

Caprice stared at the woman who had been her doctor for all the years that she had been a St. James. "I can't be. I take precautions," Caprice replied, saying the first thing that popped into her mind. She had come to the appointment more to satisfy Silke than her own need. She had expected something along the lines of a flu or virus. Not a baby.

"And nothing is foolproof. After you went off the Pill, you know we discussed the probability factor of pregnancy with the method you're using. It isn't as accurate, no matter how careful you are," the doctor reminded her gently, taking in the shock that Caprice hadn't been able to hide.

Caprice made an effort to pull herself together. "That was a stupid thing to say. I do remember what you told me," she admitted. Quin's child. Of all the ironies. She couldn't keep the man, but he had left her with a piece of himself and he didn't even know it.

The doctor stared at her for a moment, then shook her head. "You're about six weeks along." She hesitated, then added, "There are alternatives to having the child."

"No!" Caprice laced her fingers over her abdomen in an instinctively protective gesture.

Frowning at this vehemence in a woman who rarely let her emotions show, the doctor murmured, "I'm not saying that I recommend any particular course. I was just going to outline your options."

If she had been asked this morning what she would do if she was with child, she would have had any number of logical reasonings ready. But this was real. The child was real in a world that had held nothing but a gray emptiness only hours before. Quin's child. His gift. That was her reality, and logic could take a flying leap into outer space. "There is only one option. I want this baby. No matter what."

"And the father?"

Caprice didn't even have to think about her answer. She knew the honor of the man she loved. She bore its scars and now she carried its seed. "Would want it too if he knew."

The doctor masked her surprise. "You're not going to tell him?"

"I can't."

The doctor's frown deepened briefly, then changed as she absorbed the implications of Caprice's sudden, flat tone of despair. "I'm sorry, Caprice. I had no idea."

It took a second for Caprice to understand the comment. The woman believed Quin was dead. The sympathy in her eyes was unmistakable. Caprice almost opened her mouth to correct her but changed her mind at the last minute. In all the ways that counted as far as others were concerned, that was what Quin was. Dead.

"At this time, there is nothing more important to me than this baby," she said instead and with total truth.

"If you're worried about your health, don't. Right now, in spite of the morning sickness, you're fine physically. A little weary, but the pills I'll give you will help with the nausea."

"No pills. I won't take the chance."

"These won't . . ."

"I mean it. If I have to stay flat on my back until the nausea goes on its own, I will, but no pills."

"All right." She smiled faintly. "It shouldn't come to that. Just be easy with yourself. Sleep as much as you want. Gentle exercise and easy movements out of prone positions. In short, baby yourself a little." She got to her feet. "And make regular appointments with me. The next one next month."

Caprice rose and walked with the doctor to the door. "You're sure I'm all right?"

The woman smiled. "Very all right. And babies are tough little scraps of humanity. They take what they need regardless. It's the mother who pays the toll at a time like this. So stop worrying and start planning, thinking of names, and so forth."

Caprice inclined her head, not ready to smile just yet. The knowledge of the gift that Quin had given her was too new, too startling. She had thought she had lost everything and found she had a future. Not the one she prayed for, but one that held something that mattered very much. Quin's legacy, his child. She entered the waiting room, her gaze holding Silke's. Her sister stood, ready to leave. Neither spoke in the crowded elevator.

"What did she say?" Silke demanded impatiently, the moment they got into the car.

Caprice angled her body, very conscious of the embryo even now gaining strength from her being. "I'm pregnant."

Silke blinked, stared, then blinked again. "Say that one more time," she managed finally.

"I'm pregnant with Quin's child." She reached out and took Silke's hand. "Be happy for me. I thought I had lost everything, but now I have this."

Silke squeezed Caprice's fingers, stunned at the need in her sister's eyes. Her time with Quin had changed her out of all recognition. "If you want this child, you know I will do anything I can to help," she said honestly. She hesitated, then asked the question uppermost in her mind. "How are you going to tell Quin? Or are you?"

Caprice released Silke's hand and sat back in her seat. She hadn't thought that far ahead. But with the questions she had to examine her course. For herself, she would have faced Quin's danger for just the promise of one more day in his life. But for his child, the living legacy of the man, she could not risk it. In that second, she realized the depth of Quin's complete commitment to her. For her sake, he had let her go. For their child's sake, she must do the same.

"I won't tell him. He would want us both." She lifted eyes to Silke's, seeing the confusion her words had created. "I can't tell you the whole story, but Quin lives with a kind of danger that is worse than my kidnapping. I can't . . . no, I won't expose his child to that danger any more than he would allow me to continue to live under its threat. He made the choice, but I will abide by it."

Silke studied Caprice's set expression, reading a determination that wouldn't be moved by any words that she could use. "Killian isn't going to like this," she said finally. "I don't see him letting you take on this pregnancy by yourself."

"Then don't tell him."

"You can't keep this a secret. In a few weeks you're going to start showing, depending on how far along you are."

"I'm six weeks. And I know I can't keep it a secret forever. But I will for as long as I can. I've got things to do, plans to make. And above all else, no one but the family must ever hear the name of this child's father. It is the only way I can guarantee its safety and Quin's."

Silke inclined her head, understanding because of all that Killian had told her and what little she knew herself. "I'll remember." She turned on the ignition. "You do realize that half the world is going to be thinking some crazy things."

Caprice smiled faintly when she had thought she would never smile again. "I don't care. I'm just so happy I could cry. I'm not empty anymore," she said simply, the truth all the more poignant for its simplicity. "Quin is gone but he left a part of himself behind to keep me company. It is more than I thought I would have."

Silke heard the complete acceptance in Caprice's voice. She couldn't think of a time when her sister wasn't striving to attain. No challenge was too great. No goal too impossible. Yet with Quin she was not only walking away from a future with the man she loved, but accepting it as though it were right.

"I don't understand you. If you love this man whose child you carry, fight for him. Don't roll over. You never have. Neither of us has."

Caprice leaned back in the seat, lacing her fingers across her abdomen. "Let's go home, Silke," Caprice murmured, ignoring her words. "And if your offer of a place to stay is still open, I'd like to accept for a while, at least until the nausea goes."

"Don't be an ass. You're staying a lot longer than that." She guided the car into traffic, then continued with her original thoughts. "What about Quin? He has a right to know about this child even if you two don't get together," she pointed out, trying another tack. "By your own admission, he would want you both."

Caprice frowned, Silke's words making an impression. "It would change nothing in the end."

"I think you're underestimating Quin and yourself. Nobility works on paper, but it sure won't keep you warm at night, and it definitely won't give your baby a father."

"Quin's baby has a father," Caprice stated flatly, the first hint of anger entering her voice. "He or she will know Quin. I'll see to it."

Silke shot her a look, then shook her head. "I'm not giving up, you know."

"Try all you want, just don't tell Killian."

"Afraid of what he will do?"

Caprice nodded without saying anything. She was definitely worried about what Killian would do. She had seen his face too clearly when he had left her in the limo to talk to Quin for her. He didn't agree with what Quin had decided to do, nor was he happy with the part he had had to play in the clean-up. Killian had a temper, and he was completely committed to Silke and her interests. For Silke, if not for her, he would go to battle with Quin. Quin would win, but it would cost them all too much for the victory.

"If you won't go to him, write him a letter."

"I don't know the address and neither do you."

"Killian will give it to you."

Caprice smiled at her sister as she sipped her tea. "Stop nagging and get dressed. You promised to help me look at houses. I refuse to bring Quin's child up in an apartment."

"This baby is yours, too."

Caprice's smile widened into a grin. "I know, but it pleases me to think of it as his."

Silke grimaced. "I still won't give up."

"I know that, too. You like nagging. Even Killian says so."

Silke got to her feet, muttering a few choice oaths. "I never thought I would see the day when you were complacent. You've heard the expression of a contented cow. Except for the fact that your body shape looks more like an elegant greyhound's, you have a lot in common with that animal."

Caprice laughed. "Hurry up or I'll leave you."

As Caprice watched Silke leave the room, her expression changed. For the past four days she had countered every one of Silke's attempts to get her to see reason over Quin. She knew her sister was certain that Quin would take on her and the baby without hesitation and that he would convince her to agree. Caprice was equally certain that it was the one course that would destroy them. But despite all of the reasons they couldn't be together, one thing stood out. Quin did have a right to know about the baby. Her emptiness had been filled with his gift, but who or what would do the same for him? He had told her that there would be no woman like her in his life, and she believed him with every fiber of her being. His days would be an unending source of gray as hers had been. She had the power to ease that burden if she had the strength to face him one more time, to share with him the life that they had created out of the time they had stolen from reality. She stroked her still-flat stomach, feeling stronger than she had ever felt in her life. She could do it. Quin had been wise enough to face their future and make an impossible choice. She would match that power with her own version. She would give him back the gift that he had offered her.

Silke stalked back into the kitchen, her handbag slung from a strap on her shoulder. "All right. I'm ready."

Caprice rose. "Good. I want to make a detour before we meet with the realtor."

"Where?"

"Killian's office. You're right. I do want Quin to know."

Silke's face cleared as if by magic as she searched Caprice's expression. "You mean it. Finally, you're talking sense."

Caprice smiled faintly. Silke foresaw a happy ending with her and Quin raising their child. Caprice didn't bother to correct her. Reality would do that better than she ever could.

Fifteen

"I can't believe my bullheaded husband refused to give you Quin's address," Silke muttered angrily. "You should have told him you were pregnant. Or let me."

"No. We've been over this. Quin is going to know first."

"*I* know."

"Only because you were there that day." Caprice stared out the window, thinking hard. "Are you sure you don't know where Quin's island is?"

"Not enough to give you an address. All I know for certain is that, we landed in Nassau overnight and then the next morning a seaplane came from the island to take us the rest of the way."

"How long did you fly?"

"A little less than an hour."

"Where was the sun?"

Silke grimaced as she tried to remember. "I was on my honeymoon, damn it. I don't know."

Caprice turned her head to look at her. "Think, Silke. You know what's at stake. Help me."

"I'm trying. I want you to have this man if he matters this much. I want you to know what I have with Killian. But I'm not good with directions. I never have been." She swore again graphically, then pulled up her memories, focusing on the plane even as she guided the car home. With Killian's refusal, Caprice had lost interest in house hunting. Finding Quin took precedence.

"Sort of on the left," she said finally.

"South." Caprice considered that for a second. "We need a map and someone who knows about that area."

"A travel agent."

"Worth a shot."

Two hours later, a couple of long-distance phone calls, and one very happy fledgling agent who had just managed to make a connection with the wealthy St. James family gave Silke and Caprice a lead.

"Okay. We know the area. Now what?" Silke demanded.

"You and I are going to the airport. And you're going to vamp someone into giving us the flight plan for that day and Quin's plane."

"We know where it was going."

"True, but I don't know a thing about flight plans and neither do you. For all we know the final destination of the connecting flight may be on it."

It wasn't. But the man that Silke vamped just happened to know someone in the Nassau airport and just happened to want to impress Silke and just happened to get the destination of the seaplane that had taken Silke and Killian to the island.

"I don't believe it," Silke crowed, grinning as she slipped into the car. "We actually got it. Killian is going to be fit to be tied when he finds out."

"He isn't going to find out," Caprice reminded her.

"I know. I still think I should go with you."

"No. I need to do this alone."

Silke sighed, worried in spite of the elation at having gotten the formation they had spent all day hunting. "You're sure?" She glanced at her sister.

Caprice nodded. She had made her decision. There was no going back, even if she wanted to. She had found Quin's lair and he deserved to know about his child. That as all that mattered in this moment. All she would allow to matter. The consequences of her choices would be dealt with when and as they came. "With the flight out tonight, the most I will be gone is three days. The baby and I will be fine."

Because Caprice was certain, Silke found herself relaxing slightly . "You'd better be. I don't want to explain to the family how I let you risk yourself. They still haven't recuperated from the kidnapping."

"Have I told you how much I appreciate . . ."

Silke interrupted her ruthlessly. "If you love me, don't go mushy on me. Just knock some sense into Quin or let him knock some into you. I don't want my sister to end up without the man she loves."

Killian glanced at the paperwork in front of him. He would much rather have been at home with Silke in spite of having Caprice in his apartment, but he was waiting for a call, a call he definitely didn't want to take. He transferred his gaze to the phone, willing it to ring for the sheer pleasure of giving one Randall Quinlan hell. Nearly a week of watching Caprice try to function was enough to put him off his feed. And now this latest development. Since Silke had made her go to that damn doctor, Caprice had changed yet again. Then on top of that, she now had some crazy idea about following Quin to his island. Knowing his wife and her sister, he didn't put much store in their accepting his refusal to give them the information they had sought. He didn't know how either of them could find Quin, but he was more than sure they would try. So he had done what he promised himself he wouldn't do and contacted Quin, or at least tried to.

Suddenly the phone obeyed his will and rang. Killian snatched it up and spoke his name tersely.

"What is it?" Quin asked without a greeting.

Killian scowled at the tone. "What it is, is your woman's trying to get to you."

Quin's stomach clenched into a knot of rejection. "Like hell."

"Definitely like that. I put a spoke in her wheel by refusing to give her your address, but she seems determined and she has Silke's help."

Quin swore long and hard. "Stop her," he commanded roughly, thinking of all his plans, the hunters who were even now closing in on his retreat.

"You tell me how, short of tying her up," Killian shot back equally abruptly.

"I don't care how you do it, just get it done. The woods are full of hunters and there is only one buck here."

It was Killian's turn to swear. "How soon?"

"Best estimate, two days. Maybe less. Stall her. Anything. But don't let her out of your sight."

"How bad?"

"End of the road one way or another," Quin stated flatly.

Killian said nothing for a second as he absorbed the analysis. "Can I help?"

Quin recognized the depth of respect, even liking, in Killian's question. He had stretched their association to the limits with his treatment of Caprice and the way he had kept Killian in the dark with his handling of the pseudo assassination. But still Killian offered his support, "Just keep her safe. More than that doesn't matter."

"I'll handle it." He listened to the gentle buzz of the broken connection in his ear. Whatever hell Caprice was facing, so, too, was Quin. Both alone, both committed, but too aware of what the price of their relationship would be. Suddenly, the paperwork didn't seem so important after all. Silke was waiting. For him, because of Quin, there was a happy ending.

"Are you sure you're going to be all right?" Silke demanded worriedly. "You can still change your mind. I can get a ticket right now."

"You don't have any luggage."

Silke shrugged gracefully, a smile lightening the gravity of her expression for a moment. "I never have any trouble shopping. Killian swears you could put me down in a desert and I would find a Saks in two minutes."

Caprice laughed softly as she knew Silke intended she should. Hearing the announcement of her flight, she got to her feet. "I'll be fine. I promise. The morning sickness seems to be on temporary hold and I have only one lay-over between here and Nassau."

"But no guarantee of a seaplane at the end of it unless I can pull off a miracle."

Caprice leaned forward to hug her briefly. "Stop worrying," she said as she stepped back. "I can handle it."

Silke glared as the final announcement was given. "All right. But remember, you call me if you have any trouble at all. I'll be out of here on the next flight if I have to charter a plane to do it."

Caprice nodded and headed for the boarding tunnel. There was no more to say, and as much as she loved her sister, her thoughts weren't on Silke. She had no room for anyone but Quin, and the child that even now was growing within her. She had nothing but her faith in him on which to base her belief that he would care that she held his seed in her womb. She had nothing but her love to give her the strength to face him after he had sent her away. Would it be enough? She prayed for all their sakes that she would not come up short. Her child's future lay in her hands.

"You did what?"

Silke glared at her husband, her hands on her hips. "I said I helped Caprice find out where Quin's island is. And then we came back here, packed her a bag, and I took her to the airport. She's in the air and there is nothing you or he can do to stop her seeing him. He owes her this, damn it, and you know it."

Killian raked his fingers through his hair, remembering too well the urgency in Quin's voice when he had thought Caprice might come to him. "How long ago?" he demanded impatiently.

Silke stared at him. She had expected anger, even irritation at the way she and Caprice had outfoxed him. She hadn't expected undisguised anxiety. "About an hour, give or take ten minutes."

Killian strode to the phone, dialed the number he knew by memory, and waited for it to be answered. "Get him," he said tersely when an unknown voice replied. "It's Killian."

"Hold."

Killian grimaced, staring at Silke as she waited, her expression changing with every second. He wanted to reassure her, but he was out of lies for the task. He held out his hand. She came to him, wrapping her arms around his waist. He hugged her briefly just as Quin came on the line. Because Silke was so close she was able to hear the exchange and draw enough conclusions to fan her fear. Caprice was at risk and so was the child neither man knew she was carrying. She knew her sister. She would do whatever it took to keep that baby alive.

"She's flying. She was gone by the time I got home."

Quin didn't waste time swearing. "Get out here, ASAP. Not for me. Her. No time. I'd intercept her in Nassau if it weren't more dangerous for her to be out in the open. I'll have the seaplane meet her, then send it back for you."

"I'll be on it."

"Connection there?"

"The best." With the answer he hung up. "Help me pack."

"I'm coming, too."

"No. I don't have time to argue. Caprice is walking into hell and she isn't immortal." Even as he spoke he entered the bedroom and stalked to the closet to pull out a few clothes with one hand while he snagged the phone with the other. Dialing his father-in-law, he asked for and got the corporate jet.

Silke pulled out her suitcase and quickly transferred his clothes. She didn't waste time fighting a lost cause. There were other ways to win. She saw him off in less than ten minutes. Then she grabbed her coat and shot out of the apartment. Killian had always said she drove like a suicide mission pilot. She was never more glad of that streak of recklessness as she wove her way through the traffic, shaving minutes off the trip with every harebrained chance. She beat Killian to the airport. Now all she had to do was sneak onto the plane. Maybe the fates had decided to be kind. But for whatever reason, she had a clear path to the aircraft and the small facilities closet at the rear. Praying as she rarely did, she pressed her ear against the door. It seemed like only seconds after she heard Killian come aboard that they were airborne. Breathing a sigh of relief, she sat down to wait until she was sure Killian wouldn't turn back.

"Are you certain this seaplane is for me?" Caprice asked, staring at the slim man in front of her. Silke had said she would keep trying to arrange a flight from her end, but Caprice hadn't expected her to succeed. She should have known better.

The pilot inclined his head. "It is for you," he agreed as he bent to lift the single case she had brought with her. "You will come with me?"

"All right," Caprice followed him to the small, squat aircraft crouched on the tarmac. Weariness was dragging at her, but she was almost at the end of her journey. In less than an hour, she would see Quin. She settled into her seat, snapped the seat belt in place, and folded her hands over her abdomen. For the first time since she and Silke had begun this chase, she felt nervous. Quin was such a complicated man. She had made her decision, but there was no guarantee that he would agree. What if he insisted on marriage? Could she be strong enough to resist the temptation of something she wanted so very much? So many questions and not one answer in sight.

And as they drew closer to the island, the doubts, the needs, the unfulfilled dreams didn't gentle. Instead, they dug in with claws to tear at her control. The nausea returned and she fought that with the same determination she fought her fears. While the plane plowed through the dark water to bring her to Quin's island, she stared into the night wrapped like an inky shroud around her chariot. Quin waited in that darkness. Would he fill it with his own special warmth, or would she feel only the emptiness that had lived since he had touched her that one last time?

"You're sure he's that close?"

"There is no mistake, Rom. Gustaf has taken the bait just as you knew he would," Quin's second-in-command said. He tipped his head, listening. "The plane has landed."

"I hear it," Quin admitted without turning to look into the darkness for the flash of landing lights that told him Caprice was near. "Meet it. Take her to the salon and keep her there. I have to set the last pieces of the chess game." So few minutes to share with his woman and couldn't take the risk until he had the final plans in motion.

The second nodded, his dark eyes more concerned than his expression showed. "You have planned well. It will work."

"Gustaf rarely loses."

"He will this time."

Quin picked up the phone. "We shall see. Either way. All of us will be free."

The man met his look, each aware that death brought its own kind of freedom. "As you say. We cannot lose."

Caprice paced the opulent room without bothering to try the door that she had found to be locked the moment she had stepped into the salon. She should have been angry. It had been almost an hour since the polite man who had identified himself as Quin's second had shown her where to wait. But she was too nervous to be angry. Something was very wrong. She could feel it in the air. In many ways, the sensations feathering over her skin reminded her of the night that she had been taken by Gustaf. She wrapped her arms around herself as she stared at the wall of paintings that brought life to the beautiful, elegant room. In another time, she could have found pleasure in the visual delight of the treasures in Quin's home.

Quin opened the door silently, stepped inside, and closed it just as soundlessly. For a moment, he allowed himself the luxury of looking at her. She seemed thinner, yet it had only been a little over a week since he had last touched her. But she was still as exquisite as he remembered, maybe even more so. Her back was tempered steel, her strength in her bearing, the regal tilt of her chin. His warrior maid. He was counting on her strength. He needed it more than he could or would tell her. It was her salvation, perhaps even his own. His hands clenched into fists at his sides as he braced himself to do what had to be done. To save her, he had to kill whatever need had driven her to seek him out. Time was just too short for gentleness and reason. Gustaf was closing in and the final game was about to begin. The stakes were all or nothing.

"You don't listen very well," he said roughly as he walked toward her.

Caprice whirled around, her eyes widening at the first sight of him. His eyes glittered like polished steel. His tread was that stride of barely leashed menace that both intrigued and frightened. He was dressed all in black. A stranger in a body that she had known in passion, desire white-hot and gentleness feather soft. Her lover. This stranger was the man who had touched her with such wanting that she had been branded forever. This stranger had left his seed within her to be nurtured by her and the love she bore him.

"I meant what I said in Houston. There is no room in Randall Quinlan's life for you. It's too damn dangerous." Every word was a stake driven into his own heart. He absorbed each blow and came back for more. He would bleed later, if there was a later.

Caprice hardly heard him. The change in him was too dramatic, too telling. Suddenly, the last piece of the equation that was Quin fell into place. This is what he had tried to tell her when he had said she could not tread his world at his side. This man gave no quarter because in his world that was a death sentence. He was diamond-hard clear to his soul and in that lay his greatest defense. For her, he had been gentle, a lover, a man capable of feeling, needing, and wanting. For their child, he would give that and more. But in the giving, she might as well put a gun to his head. It was that simple, that irrefutable, and that inescapable.

Suddenly that gift she had come to share was no gift. Rather a curse without an end.

"No comeback?" he mocked, stopping a kiss's breath away from her. Her scent surrounded him, sheer torture for a man already strung on the rack of his own making.

"I shouldn't have come," she said quietly, loving him as she had yet to do. She now knew the full extent of his scarring from the past, and, as when she had seen the visible disfigurements, she didn't turn away. Her kiss would not soothe these brands of time and experience, but her silence could offer a solace of which only she would know the source; but he would feel it.

"No, you shouldn't have. Had I wanted you here, I would have made a place," he said, driving the point home to the bone. His silent shout of agony was the scream of a man too strong to bend. "But don't worry. You won't be here long." He cocked his head. "In fact, that should be Killian right now." He gestured toward the door. "I'll walk you out."

Caprice studied him for a second, once again aware of something more than just his need for her to be gone. The Caprice who had landed would have asked. This one looked, felt the bite of curiosity, then turned from it. He had given her all he could. And she had taken that, giving all she could in return. Wishes and dreams weren't and never would be real.

"As you ask," she murmured, her lashes closing for one brief second.

Quin lifted his hand, then let it drop. To touch her was to risk more than he had a right to expect or take. He stepped back. Caprice moved past him into the hall. No one spoke, not the men they walked by or Quin. Caprice kept her eyes on the dock she could barely see. It was the bridge between his world and her own, a fragile thing made by human hands, easily destroyed. She hesitated at the meeting of land and human creation. She glanced at Quin.

"If you love me, no farther. This is your place. That plane is part of mine. You were right. Neither of us can live with the other, for the only place we could make would be as flimsy, as prey to danger as this dock."

Quin inhaled deeply, hearing his own words whispered in the voice that had once spoken of need and love. The prophecy had promised she would slay his dragons. But it had never promised that he would live to see the last one fall or that she would be his forever.

"I wish it could be different."

She smiled, so many emotions in the single gesture that no one was stronger than the other.

"I don't. I love you as you are. Here or somewhere else. I told you that once before. I still mean it now, even when you tried to hurt me to make me leave."

He stiffened as he realized she had seen more than he wanted her to know. "Don't read something that is not there."

She shook her head and turned from him. The plane was at the end of the dock, the door open. Killian was stepping out. "Your mistake has always been in thinking I don't know you." She looked back at him. "If we had had time, I would have proved it to you." She touched his face, tracing the line of his lips. "Don't think of me in your jungle. If I could give you amnesia, I would, my love." Going on her tiptoes, she kissed him quickly, then turned and walked swiftly toward the waiting plane. Tears stood in her eyes, but not one fell—not for him, not for herself, and not for the child she would raise with love enough for the father he would not know.

Sixteen

Caprice leaned back in the cushions, aware of Silke watching her as though she expected her to fall apart at any moment. It had been this way since she had gotten into the seaplane just over an hour ago. Killian had said little beyond asking if she was all right. Instead he had retreated to the cockpit, apparently to give her and Silke privacy if she needed to talk. He had done the same thing when they had transferred to their father's aircraft.

"Did you tell him?" Silke asked finally.

Caprice turned her head, her eyes holding her sister's. "No."

"Damn men. Sometimes they don't let a woman open her mouth. They're so certain they have all the answers," Silke muttered, thinking not only of Quin but of her own stubborn male. Her ears were still ringing from his lecture on the stupidity of stowing away on the plane. Only the fact that he was as worried about Caprice as she was had kept him from continuing his comments on her reckless behavior.

Caprice smiled faintly at Silke's belligerence, guessing the cause. "It wasn't like that."

"Next you'll be telling me you changed your mind."

"I did."

Silke stared at her. "Why?" she demanded at last.

"Because he was no longer the man who loved me in Houston," she murmured ambiguously. She knew her sister. If there was a chance that Quin could be made to change his mind, Silke would fight for it. She wouldn't understand what Caprice had seen and accepted. To stop her, Caprice chose the only course available beyond creating the lie of no longer loving Quin. That she just couldn't do and carry it off with any degree of success.

Silke frowned. "He threw you out."

"He tried but I left on my own," she replied in perfect truth.

Silke swore one of her more lurid oaths, then glanced toward the cockpit in case Killian had heard. It wasn't the curse he minded so much but that she was upset enough to use it. Caprice didn't need his interference at this point.

"Now what?" she asked gently, forcing the anger from her mind. Caprice and the baby were her concerns. Quin could go to hell in his own handbasket with her blessings.

"Now, I go home. We house hunt and I have the most beautiful baby in Philly." She stroked her flat stomach, using the image of the child to warm her. The vision wasn't as perfect as the heat in Quin's embrace, but it was better by far than the cold of being alone.

Silke touched the hand lying on Caprice's stomach. "Since you say you want to do natural childbirth, can I be the coach?"

Caprice looked at her sister, the gleaming fingernails without a chip, the wild tumble of sexy curls, the glittering sultry eyes, and found a smile. "I can just see you doing it. The whole delivery room will be in stitches."

Silke shrugged, grinning. She would have braved anything to see Caprice happy again. "I figure it will be good practice for Killian and me. I'll know both sides, and I can tell him what he does wrong."

Caprice laughed softly as she tipped her head back, letting her lashes close. "You just want to get even. I know you."

"There is that," Silke murmured quietly as she sat in the silence, holding Caprice's hand until she slept. When Caprice's even breathing finally confirmed her rest, Silke eased her hand free and got up.

Killian glanced at her as she entered the cockpit area. "How is she?"

"Sleeping."

Killian nodded, then rose. "I'll be in the back for a while," he told the pilot.

Silke slipped into one of the two seats far enough away from Caprice not to disturb her. Killian looked at Caprice for a long moment before he sat down beside Silke. "What did she tell you?"

"Not much. It seems that Quin tried to throw her off the island, but she left instead."

"He's worried. And she shouldn't have come here."

"That's a mild word for what I feel. And you don't know the whole story."

Killian's eyes narrowed. "Meaning?"

"Meaning she's pregnant," she said bluntly. "That's why I stowed away. She didn't want you to know. That's why she's been so sick. I was afraid for her, and I wasn't sure she would tell you about the baby. Or what Quin would do. Or what you would do if you thought you were keeping her safe."

Killian sighed deeply, the last of his anger dying as the full ramifications sank in. "You couldn't tell me?"

"I promised her I wouldn't. She wanted Quin to be the first to know."

"I can't believe he didn't do something beyond trying to get rid of her. At the very least I would have expected him to demand I wrap her in cotton batting."

"She didn't tell him."

He nodded, remembering too well how worried Quin had sounded and the urgency that had been driving him. "It would have been better if he had shut up long enough to listen."

"It wasn't that either."

"You're not making sense."

"Neither is she."

Killian glanced over his shoulder. "What do you want me to do?"

"Find out what's going on," she replied promptly.

"Can't."

Silke's eyes narrowed. "What does that mean?"

Keeping in mind what his wife could do and had done when she was thwarted in trying to help Caprice, Killian decided on honesty. "That means Quin is expecting big trouble. He's got some old enemies hot on his tail and he doesn't want Caprice caught in the cross fire. That's why I was so damn furious with you for stowing away. We flew right into the middle of the mess. I was to get Caprice out. Not bring you into the line of fire."

Silke stared at him, reading the fear that lived in his eyes for her and for Caprice. She looked over her shoulder to Caprice.

"Don't even think about telling her. He was very specific."

"She's not showing it but she has to be hurting. Caprice isn't a woman for an affair with little or no emotional involvement, and she sure wouldn't be having this baby if she didn't care for him even now. You know what her life was like before Quin. She was on the fast track."

"You can't make this right, Silke." He stroked her wild hair back from her cheeks, his expression gentle. "I thought when he went after her he just might be able to make it work. But the risks are too great and he got a firsthand look at the danger he was putting her in. I know what I would have felt if it had been you. I would have done what he did. There is no other choice."

"I would have followed you."

He smiled faintly. "It wouldn't have mattered. For your sake I would have kept pushing you away until you stayed."

"Then you're saying he loves her."

"Too much. Just as she loves him."

Tears filled her eyes. "Damn. She deserves her happy ending."

He pulled her close. "We can't give it to her. But we can love her as much as we can. It won't be the same, but at least she won't be as alone as he is."

Quin watched the sun rise from his vantage point on the small hill at the back of the compound. The trap was set. Offshore he could see the sleek craft riding gently on the sea. Men were moving across her decks, small ants of humanity with one goal in mind. The hunt was about to begin. The woods were full of friendlies and the seas alive with the enemy. No quarter would be given. His eyes glittered with purpose. The stage had been set for this confrontation a long time ago. He had not made the rules of this game. Gustaf had begun it, but he would finish it for all time. All debts would be paid before the day surrendered to night once more.

"Looks like he's coming ashore on the third wave," his second said softly, his binoculars to his eyes.

"Gustaf always did play it safe." Quin lifted his arm in a silent signal.

The man slipped the binoculars meticulously into their case and set it aside. He checked the clip in his weapon. "It's been a long road. The odds were it would always end like this. Only a stupid man would have stayed as long as I did."

Quin glanced at him smiling with the first real amusement he had allowed himself in this guise. "As you say, only a stupid man."

His second glared at him for a moment, then grinned, his usually serious eyes lighting with the joy of the battle to come. He had been bred in the deserts of the east where a life was less valuable than a teaspoon of water. His ancestors were nomads, warriors who to this day rode horses bred to fight and win. "See you in hell, my friend," he laughed, crawling away to his post.

Quin watched him go. Around him were only ten men, people he had come to count on over the years. They, like him, had come from hard schools, had been taught lessons that had few places in the modern world. And like him, they had chosen to retire rather than to lose their honor to the highest bidder instead of the one they felt was right. They were a strange group. No common nationality. No common political system. No common age. The only thing they shared was a need to be free, to live without looking over their shoulders. On the island they had found such a life. This was the only home most of them had had since they had turned from boys to men. And now it was threatened by the very world that bred them. They, like him, had no choice but to fight for as long as they were able and as hard as they could.

* * *

Killian closed the door to his office, crossed to his desk, and slipped out of his jacket. He was tired. It seemed like more than three days since he had left this office and rushed home to discover Caprice had flown. The problems hadn't ended when he had returned with Silke and Caprice. Caprice had faced her parents with her pregnancy, and he had sustained a politely angry interview with Geoffrey over the fact that he had known who and what Quin was and made no effort to stop him from contacting Caprice. It hadn't helped that Caprice had discovered what her father had said and done. He still wasn't sure how. He had certainly told no one. That had been yesterday. By last night, Silke was involved. Caprice was angry. Geoffrey was tight-lipped, and Lorraine looked so guilty about the whole thing that Killian wasn't sure who was going to break first.

He dropped into his chair, glared at the paperwork stacked in front of him, and wondered if life would return to normal anytime soon. Suddenly the intercom buzzed. He punched the appropriate button.

"There's a Mr. Emil Valdais on line one," his secretary murmured.

"Did he say what he wanted?"

"Something about a Randall Quinlan."

Killian's eyes narrowed. "I'll take it," he said quickly before breaking the interoffice connection and tapping into line one.

"I shall get right to the point," Valdais said after introducing himself. "I am Randall Quinlan's lawyer. I am afraid I have bad news for you. I understand you are a friend of Mr. Quinlan, so I must apologize for what I am about to say. As of three o'clock yesterday your time, Mr. Quinlan was killed. Apparently his island was attacked by some mercenaries and most of the area was destroyed. There were no survivors. Even those who had come were all killed. The police have been over there and confirmed the events."

Killian said nothing for a moment, thinking of what he would have to tell Caprice. On top of all she had been through, he didn't know how she would take the announcement. "What else?" he asked finally.

"Mr. Quinlan left an estate, quite a substantial one. You are the executor, and the beneficiary is a woman named Caprice St. James. I am told that you will take care of conveying this news to Ms. St. James."

"I will." The fact that Quin had named Caprice as his heir meant that his will was very new.

"I can't give you the exact details as yet on all his assets. I'm still waiting for some confirmations since this last change. But I will get the paperwork to you as soon as possible."

"You have my address."

"Yes. Mr. Quinlan was most thorough."

"He would be."

The lawyer sighed deeply. "You knew him well, I think. He was well thought of in this area by the few of us who knew him at all. He was a man who dealt fairly. He should not have had the kind of enemies who would do such a thing."

"I will tell Ms. St. James what you said. It will mean a lot to her," he replied. After saying all the expected things he hung up the phone, got to his feet, and shrugged back into his jacket. Dialing his home, he waited, hoping Silke would be the one to pick up the phone.

"Good, you're still there."

"We were just on our way to the realtor's."

"Can you stall?"

Silke frowned at Killian's tone. "Something's wrong?" She glanced hurriedly over her shoulder, keeping watch in case Caprice walked into the kitchen.

"Very."

"Quin?"

"I'll tell you both when I get there."

"We'll be waiting."

"Silke, will you get a move on? I thought you said you liked those shoes with that dress," Caprice said.

"I did," Silke muttered from the depths of her closet. If Killian didn't hurry, Caprice was going to get suspicious. "The thing is I just remembered they're a witch to walk in all day. And I bet you my best earrings that you'll be dragging me through every house that woman has on her list. I am not coming home with blisters. And if I change my shoes, I have to change my dress."

"And your makeup and your jewelry. And your hairstyle," Caprice finished with a sigh that was half amused and half irritated. "I'll call the realtor."

"And I'll hurry," Silke replied, lying without a qualm.

Caprice moved to the bedside stand and made her call. By the time she hung up, Silke was still in the closet. "I'm going to the living room and put my feet up. I don't think I want to watch this fashion show."

"Good idea."

Caprice waited for a second, then left. Minutes ticked slowly by. A sound came from the hall. She glanced over her shoulder just as Silke came out of her bedroom, wearing the same clothes that she had sworn she was going to change. Before Caprice could comment, Killian came into the room. One look at his face and she felt the first touch of fear.

"What is it?" she asked as her hands curled protectively around her abdomen.

Silke sat down beside her on the couch. Killian took the chair across from her.

"Not good."

"Quin?" she demanded swiftly.

He nodded. "There is no easy way, Caprice. I wish there were. He's dead."

Caprice didn't say a word. She couldn't. She simply felt. First the fear, the lurch of her heart damming the breath that even now carried life through her body. Quin dead. Impossible. She could walk away as long as she knew he still lived. Her fingers pressed gently into her flesh as though she needed to feel the minute throb of the life he had given her to take his place.

"You're sure?"

"Gustaf attacked his island. There was a fight. Everyone was killed."

"He knew it was coming, didn't he?"

He nodded, stunned at the calm with which she was asking her questions. There were no tears in her eyes, but there were in Silke's. Caprice was pale but her breathing was easy. Shock? He edged forward on his chair, ready to catch her if she broke. "He knew."

"You knew?"

"Yes."

Caprice looked beyond him, searching her feelings. Something was not right. "He's died before. He told me," she murmured, hardly aware she spoke aloud.

Killian thought he understood. "Yes. But not this time. The kind of dying you're talking about takes time to set up. A lot more than the week he had."

"He moved mountains for me that night." She looked back at him, daring him to deny it.

"It's not the same. If I didn't believe it, I would not have told you. I checked it out with sources more reliable than the local police. It's true."

She shook her head, rejecting the words that Killian seemed to believe as true. "He doesn't feel dead to me. I would know."

Silke covered her hands, feeling the tears sliding down her face. "It's shock, Caprice."

She shook her head again. "It doesn't feel like that either."

Silke glanced at Killian for help. He inclined his head toward the bedroom. "Why don't you lie down for a while? I'll call the realtor and tell her we'll make it another day."

Caprice stared at her, hearing the words, even accepting them. Not because she believed, but because she needed to be alone. "All right," she agreed docilely, getting to her feet.

She walked with Silke to the room she had been using, letting Silke cover her with a light blanket and closing her eyes as if she were going to sleep. But none of it was real. The moment the door to the room shut, she opened her eyes, tossed aside the blanket, and sat up. She stared out the window, thinking of the warrior who had confronted her on the island. That man was not dead. She wouldn't believe it if she had touched the body. He had known Gustaf was coming. He had sent her away with the fastest method at his disposal. The danger that she had sensed that night had been Gustaf's coming. Quin would have felt that danger even better than she. He would have won. No matter what Gustaf was, Quin would have won.

Somewhere in the world, under a different name, Quin lived. Her lips trembled into a smile. She would never see him again.

She wouldn't even know his new name. But he lived. As his son or daughter would live. As her love would live. The world would accept his death. She would even help it accept his death for his sake. But he lived.

Seventeen

Killian finished the last of the report he had been scanning. His business had never been better than it was these last few months. Even his home life was finally settling into a pattern now that Caprice had found herself a house in the country and the family waters had calmed after the furor of Caprice's return and Quin's death. He smiled faintly. Silke was even talking of babies, teasing him about the experience she was gaining at the natural childbirth classes she attended with Caprice. As for Caprice, she had accepted Quin's legacy, putting it into a trust fund for her child. Then she had set about creating a home for the baby. She had lost her taste for the fast lane to the shock of everyone but Silke. Instead, she seemed content if not happy enough to smile. If she thought of Quin these days, no one but she knew it.

Suddenly the buzz of his interoffice line interrupted his thoughts. "Killian, Darian McCloud is here for his four o'clock appointment."

Killian glanced at his watch. It was closer to five. "Send him in," he murmured, controlling his impatience. If he hadn't heard of the man who had a reputation for being a kind of Howard Hughes and known of his far-flung business, including his newest dip into the world of breeding Arabian horses, he would have been less polite. He had come far enough in his field not to have to put up with just any kind of behavior from a client.

The door to his office opened. The man walked in. Killian studied him. His hair was so black that it seemed to have blue highlights to match the shrewd blue of his eyes. He was a big man, easily touching the six foot five or six mark. His stride was that of a man accustomed to command and to physical work. He smiled easily as he held out his hand. The handshake was firm but with calluses to reinforce the impression of a man who knew hard labor intimately.

"I apologize for being late," Darian said as he took a seat. The slight southwestern drawl was easy, slightly amused.

Killian sighed, deciding, without knowing specifically why, that he liked this man. Maybe it was the straight, you-can-trust-me look in his eyes that did it. "I wouldn't recommend making a habit of it."

Darian laughed, his eyes glittering with humor and acceptance of the reprimand. "I hate impunctuality, too. Damn inconvenient when you're running a business."

"Especially when you have a wife at home with a party for her relatives tonight," Killian added, smiling slightly.

"I wouldn't know about that part. I'm not married yet."

Killian sat back in his chair. "Now, what can I do for you?"

Darian accepted the change of subject and began to outline his business needs. Killian made a few notes, his mind ticking over with ways and means. The minutes sped by. His secretary tapped on the door to let him know that she was leaving. Neither of them did more than pause in the exchange of information. Killian glanced at his watch as he finished the last notation. Then looked up. Suddenly his eyes narrowed. The man who had entered the room was not the same one he was looking at now.

Quin said nothing, just waited, as he had been waiting for the secretary to leave. He had taken the latest appointment he could get and then been deliberately tardy in arriving just for these moments of privacy. "Figured it out yet?" he asked quietly at last in a voice that had little trace of the drawl he had spent months perfecting.

Killian recognized the voice as he had failed to recognize the man. "The plastic surgeon did a good job," he replied finally, stunned at the changes a few months could make.

Quin held up his hands. "Even to the fingertips."

Killian hardly glanced at the gesture. His whole focus was the face of the man who had once been Quin. "If you weren't already dead, I would kill you myself," he growled, thinking of all he, Silke, Caprice, and everyone else had gone through for the past few months. "Why are you here?"

Quin's brows rose as he heard the demand that he had expected. Even he hadn't been sure he could pull off the impossible. "For Caprice. In the open. Safe. A real courtship under the eyes of her family and anyone who cares to look. Then marriage and we'll settle down to raise Arabs and babies. And not one shadow of the past on the horizon."

"You think I would let you get within a mile of her?"

Quin smiled gently, not one hint of the gypsy in the gesture. But there was a rock-hard determination that would brook no interference. "You won't stop me. She won't either, although she might try at first."

"You don't know what you did to her."

His amusement died, his eyes suddenly reflecting the hell he had lived with for seven long months of plans, operations, and lessons to change every aspect of his existence as he reconstructed a past, present, and future that would withstand any scrutiny and give Caprice the life she should have.

Killian read the cost in the look. He sighed deeply, thinking of the way Caprice had finally settled to making a home for her child and herself. Only in the last month had the family begun to relax a little, to believe she was pulling out of the strange mood that had held her in its grip for long weeks after the announcement of Quin's death.

"I know. Better than you probably."

"You weren't here."

"I am now. You won't drive me out. Only she can send me away."

"Why did you come to me?"

"To see if the new me would hold. But more I want you to arrange for me to see her. I don't want to drop in on her. She might need her people around her."

"You understand that and you still put her through believing you were dead."

"And I would again to give her our future. She is stronger than you believe. Tell me she collapsed."

Killian swore at the challenge he couldn't refute. "You know she didn't."

Quin leaned back in his chair. Only facing Caprice would be harder than confronting Killian. "When will you arrange it?"

Killian got to his feet, pacing to the window to look out. "I didn't say I would."

"You will, for her sake."

He swung around, glaring. "Don't push it. You hurt Silke too, damn you."

"It was necessary."

"No apologies?"

"You would not make them."

Killian swore again, knowing the truth even if he didn't like it. "No. I wouldn't make them. And I would also face the devil himself for a chance with Silke, so I understand that, too. But don't hurt Caprice again or I'll come after you with a dull knife. But before I do anything, I want to know what happened on the island and how you can be sure you're safe now."

Quin inclined his head, expecting no less. "The island was a natural trap as well as a fortress. When I had the compound built, I had certain routes added that provided me and those with me a way out. I could not allow Gustaf to live. His debt total had exceeded his assets, and certain people, the kind who once hired you, wanted him out of the picture. In return they would provide my associates with new lives."

"But not you?"

Smiling, Quin shook his head. "Do you remember the man who tricked Caprice into coming downstairs?" He waited for Killian's nod before he continued. "I counted on him being with the assault group. He was. He fell. Not by my hand. But he ended up being identified as me."

"Surely your people . . ."

"Never saw the body at that point. The ones who had survived had already been taken out of the picture by our mutual friends. Gustaf was dead, as were his followers."

"And Darian McCloud? The man has been around a lot longer than seven months."

Quin laughed softly, deeply. "A whim. I had read a biography of your Howard Hughes. His secrecy intrigued me. I decided to see if it could be done in this day of the computer. So I created Darian McCloud."

Killian searched his face, seeing nothing of the man he had known as Randall Quinlan or the men who had lived in that same body before him.

"Do I pass?"

Killian sighed deeply. If he had been asked, he would have said that Quin's resurrection was impossible. Now he knew it was not. "You know you do."

Quin leaned forward in his chair, his eyes holding Killian's. "Then you will arrange a meeting. When? Tonight?"

Killian frowned, thinking of the baby shower that would be taking place at eight o'clock. Caprice was in the city at his apartment. They would be having dinner together first, then the rest of the family and friends were coming for the shower. He focused on Darian, seeing the impatience he was making no attempt to hide. Quin would never have shown his feelings so completely.

"Caprice is coming to the apartment for dinner before a party we're giving. I don't want to do this. No matter what you have been through, her situation has been worse. I won't have her hurt. This way, she'll meet you with us around if I take you home with me as a friend of mine. At least you've changed so completely that there is no chance she'll recognize you unless you give her a clue the way you did me. But I want your word on something. No matter what you see or think, you won't do or say anything to let her know who you are and you will leave before the party."

"What if she asks me to stay?"

"She won't."

Darian examined the certainty in his voice, frowning a little. "She has another man?"

Killian shook his head. "She has had no one since you sent her away."

Darian sighed deeply. That fear had haunted him, not because he hadn't trusted her, but because he had known how deep the well of loneliness could be. He had known she lived, but she had believed him dead. She might have sought relief from the pain with another man.

"Do I have your word?"

He nodded. "I will do nothing, no matter what I see or think. I am only a man you took pity on."

Killian reached for his jacket. Pity might be the word for Darian before the night was over. He didn't know what he would do when he saw Caprice and the baby that made a pumpkin mound of her stomach.

* * *

Caprice leaned back in the chair as she waited for Silke to return from checking on the last details before dinner. Tonight her family and friends were coming together to celebrate with her the coming birth of her child. The seven days' wonder of her pregnancy with no father had faded. These days no one asked about the father she had never publicly named, and her family never mentioned Quin's name in any way. His safety and his child's were guaranteed with those precautions, not that she told her parents or younger sisters that. They believed she had accepted his death.

"I wish you would at least get excited," Silke announced as she came back into the living room and dropped into a chair. "Just think. Only two or three more weeks and that little tummy of yours will turn into a gorgeous baby," Silke said with a grin.

Caprice sipped at her fruit juice, laughing at Silke's expectant expression. "I think you get as much fun out of my not so little belly as I do."

"I can't wait," she replied truthfully. "I had no idea how intricate the whole process is. I keep hoping I'll get into your interesting condition soon."

"Just keep practicing."

Silke's eyes smoldered with memories. "Oh we are, believe me." She tipped her head, hearing Killian's key in the lock. "Here comes my lord and master."

Caprice laughed easily, Silke's tone too blatantly false for anything less. She glanced toward the door in time to see a second man enter the room behind Killian. She hesitated, her hand half lifting her glass to her lips. She had lived with the emptiness of Quin's absence so long that the sudden warmth that only Quin could have brought to her was a shock. Her skin paled as she stared at the stranger. Nothing about him was Quin. But her body knew what her eyes didn't see. Without even realizing it, she set the glass aside and rose, her skin flushing with heat, vividly alive with the knowledge that grew stronger with every step she took toward him. She didn't see Silke's odd look or the way Killian moved out of her path. Her vision was filled with only one man, this man with the eyes of a stranger and the feel of her lover.

Quin stared at her as she walked toward him. She glowed. There was no other word for it. Her hair shone with a silver light that seemed to embrace her whole body. She was ripe with child, woman personified in the serenity of her expression and her regal bearing. She came to him on silent feet, her eyes holding his without a flicker of uncertainty. She knew him. The knowledge slipped past every defense he had. He didn't know how. He didn't know why but she knew him. She had told him that a lifetime ago and he hadn't believed her, but he did now. Looking into the green of the eyes that had always accepted the darkness with the light, he found the home he had lost before he was born. His gaze drifted gently to her stomach, to the womb that even now nourished his child. Awed by her gift, humbled by her faith, he stood waiting.

"Killian, what's going on?" Silke whispered. "Who that?"

"Look at Caprice's face and tell me who it is," he murmured back.

Silke looked and suddenly understood. Caprice had always been beautiful but it was a cool perfection. Not tonight. There was fire in her now, a fire smoldering with every step she took closer to the stranger who must be Quin. There was an eagerness in her movements, energy sizzling as though it had lain dormant until just this moment. Stunned, Silke watched the two coming together, chills racing down her spine. "He didn't die. She said he didn't die," she murmured, barely aware that she spoke.

Without saying anything, Killian wraps his arm around her shoulders and urged her out of the room. Caprice and Quin had come too far to share this moment with anyone else.

Neither Caprice nor Quin heard or noticed the others leaving.

Caprice stopped in front of Quin, her eyes running over him for one second before her fingers traced his lips. He was beautiful, the new face a work of art—strong, clean-lined, with none of the markings of the harsh experiences of his past. Man's hand had erased what man's cruelty had drawn in his features. Her gaze moved lower. The scars on his wrists and hands were no more. He was fresh, new, all things that could not be but yet were. She looked up into his deep blue eyes, seeing the contacts that hid the silver color. His hair was ebony, black as the night that had been hers since he left. Only his height was the same, just perfect for her.

Quin held her look as he reached out, his hands cupping the swollen curve of her womb, tracing the ripeness of the body he had known so intimately, touching his unborn child for the first time. Wonder, an alien emotion, darkened his eyes.

Caprice stared at his face. Where Quin had hidden his feelings, this man gave. His joy, his amazement and awe at her pregnancy were written clearly for her to share. The warmth intensified, the cold dying in the heat of the love that hadn't faltered. "Our child," she whispered, finally taking a share of the credit for the life they had created together.

Quin stared at her, his gaze intense, searching as he lifted one hand from the life she protected with her body to her face. He traced the elegant curve of her check, felt the silken texture of her skin, breathed the scent of her that had colored every one of his dreams since he had first seen her picture. His warrior maid. Even he had not realized her strength, her power. "How can you not hate me?"

Tears that she had never shed, even in the darkness of her night, stood in her eyes. "I told you. I know you. Even this way. I know you." She closed her eyes, leaning toward him, needing his mouth, his hands on her. "Kiss me in the darkness that is ours. Make the last of the loneliness go away forever."

Quin felt her words, her need all the way to the soul she had held in safe keeping for his return. He was whole because she loved him. He folded her close, sheltering the child and her protectively against his body. He had come through hell for her sake. He had risked death and made it work for him for her sake. He had turned from the past that would have destroyed them for her sake. Each price he had paid gladly, thinking to spare her everything. But as he tasted her lips, felt the life she nurtured moving against him, he knew his risks, his hell, had been a shared fire. She had borne his child with grace and love. She had held him close to her heart even when she had been told he was dead. And she had walked into a stranger's arms because they were the arms of the man who loved her beyond death.

He drew back, his eyes glittering with emotions that he would always share with her. There were no more secrets, no more shadows. The past was a bad dream that would never return. "I meant to court you. I have a life that you can share with me, a safe life, a good life. I came to get you, marry you, and take you home with me if you would come."

She smiled, not needing the explanation. He would not have come if he could not offer her all of himself. "Yes."

So easy when it shouldn't have been. If he spent a lifetime loving her, he would never be able to repay her faith or her trust. "How soon?"

"Tonight. This minute. It doesn't matter."

His smile matched hers—free, joyous, and loving. "No. We'll do it here. Your family will want to be there. And I want them there." He looked down at her stomach. "I love you." He raised his head, his eyes holding hers. "I would die for you."

She cupped his face, visually learning its contours. "I know. You showed me. But there will be no more deaths. Only life. Ours. Our children."

He caught her close, being exquisitely careful of her. His mouth took hers, his kiss deeper and more committed than mere words could convey. When he lifted his head, she laughed softly.

"I love that sound."

She shook her head, her amusement growing. "I just thought of something."

His brows rose. He felt on top of the world without a care. "What?"

"It might be nice if you introduced yourself. I really don't want to say 'I do' to the wrong man just because I don't know your name."

Darian tipped back his head, his laughter flowing freely. Life was good. His woman in his arms and his child held safe and secure beneath her heart. "I, wife to be, am Darian King McCloud of the McCloud Ranch in Oklahoma. But my friends call me Dare."

Her laughter joined his in silver ripples of joyous freedom. "How well named you are, Dare, my husband to be."